MW00489857

UNLIKELY
WITNESSES

Leslea Wahl

Unlikely Witnesses
Copyright 2018
Leslea Wahl

Published by
Leslea Wahl
PO Box
Littleton C0 80121
www.LesleaWahl.com

ISBN: 978-1-7329037-0-8

Cover design: Delia Latham
Editor: Delia Latham

*S*OMETIMES FIFTEEN MINUTES can make all the difference. Fifteen minutes later and he would've been gone for the day. A mere quarter of an hour...and this would've been someone else's problem.

Agent Martinez peered out his office window at the four teens being escorted into the red-brick building. Four sets of eyes darted back and forth between one another in silent dialogue, but not a single pair of lips parted. Not one kid took advantage of this last chance to communicate before they were separated, each led into a different interrogation room to await their fate.

The sizzle of anticipation that usually coursed through him with each new case proved elusive this afternoon. A new investigation, late on a Friday afternoon, warranted little enthusiasm. He should be wrapping up the week's paperwork in preparation for a weekend of fishing at his cabin, not starting a new assignment.

He took a swig of his coffee and shook his head.

Why did he have to be the lucky one assigned to this case? The weekend crew should be taking care of this. And to add insult to injury, he now had to deal with a bunch of teenagers. In his line of work, he'd yet to find a single young person who cared about anything besides themselves. They were good at partying and getting into trouble, but failed abysmally when it came to concern and consideration for others—or for the law.

With a glance at the wall clock, calculations began

spinning through his mind. If he hurried, he'd be kicking back on his porch, enjoying a cold brew and the view of the lake before the sun set. Ever since Maggie left, that's the way he preferred to spend his weekends—out of town, apart from everyone, away from his problems. His self-prescribed cure. The only living beings he wanted to see for the next two days were fish, preferably dangling from his line.

Resigned to the task at hand, he rolled his neck then snatched his notebook and recorder. Time to get this over with. Outside Interrogation Room 1, he huffed a frustrated sigh, pulled his shoulders back, and put on his game face.

Come on, Martinez, pick it up. What's behind door number one?

The girl wandering around the room turned towards him as he entered. Her long, light-brown hair cascaded over one shoulder. Jean shorts and a Colorado t-shirt shouted tourist—although, when it came Coloradans and their state pride, one could never be sure. Residents loved their state and proudly wore t-shirts and hats to prove it. Her blue gaze returned his steady one, scanning him the same way he was observing her.

He let the door swing shut then stood for a moment, employing one of his favorite techniques. Nothing made people more uncomfortable than silence. Anxious to end the awkward quiet, people often began talking, unwittingly divulging important information.

This girl glanced around the nearly barren room. "You know, this space could really use a make-over. If you painted these walls a nice shade of tan and added a few plants, maybe a painting or two…you could really warm it up in here."

His gaze went from her to the stark white walls. "No windows. Plants would die."

She shot him a look. "Have you never heard of artificial

plants? A few touches might help relax people."

"Sure, I'll get right to that. Shall we rename it the hospitality suite instead of the interrogation room?"

She held his gaze. The girl was not easily intimidated.

"Just a suggestion." Her thin shoulders raised in a shrug. "You might get more information from your perps if you make them feel comfortable. Ever hear the phrase 'you can catch more flies with honey than with vinegar'?"

A smart aleck. Fantastic. "I'll pass your advice on to the federal government."

He strode toward the center of the room and the only furniture, a metal table and chairs.

"Take a seat." He motioned to one of the empty chairs and placed his mug, recorder, and notebook on the table.

He lowered himself into a chair. She did the same, mirroring his action.

"My name's Agent Martinez."

The girl placed her right hand on the table, her fingernails tapping out a rhythm. "Do I get to make a phone call to my lawyer?"

His eyes narrowed. "You have a lawyer?"

The tapping stopped. "Yes." She lifted her chin, seeming to challenge his authority.

No wonder she seemed so calm. If she had a lawyer, she'd most likely been in trouble in the past. Good. Since she knew the drill, maybe she'd answer his questions quickly, and he could move on to the next room.

Just as he was about to begin, she scrunched her face.

"Well, I sort of do. I mean, it's my dad. He's a tax lawyer so I'm not sure how helpful he'd be. And he's in Minnesota. But I could still call him." Her self-assured features softened, making her appear much younger.

"You don't need a lawyer."

"But shouldn't an adult be present to make sure my rights aren't violated?" She tucked a wayward strand of hair behind her ear.

"You're seventeen, kid. You can be questioned without an adult present."

A tilt of her head caused the errant lock of hair to slip out again. "But that's a police policy. Is it the same when you're questioned by the Feds?"

In spite of himself, he liked her spunk. "Yes."

She bit her lip as she contemplated his answer. Finally, she nodded her consent then rested her arms on the table, interlacing her fingers. Her confident poise seemed to return. "Alright. What would you like to know?"

"Let's start with the basics." He held up his recorder to show he was recording the conversation. "Please state your name."

"Josie DelRio."

"Do you live here in Colorado, Josie?"

"No. I'm from Minnesota. Lake Forest."

"What brings you to Glenwood Springs?"

"Vacation."

"But not with your dad, who's still back in Minnesota."

She nodded, then glanced at the recorder. "Oh. Um. Right. I'm here with my boyfriend, Ryan, and his family. We came for a family vacation with his grandpa, aunt, uncle and cousins."

He flipped open his notebook. "They included you in their family reunion?"

"Well, it's kind of a long story." She leaned back and smiled...like he was an old friend she couldn't wait to catch up with. "Earlier this summer, Ryan and I worked at a summer camp with his cousin and her boyfriend. We had a blast, so when Ryan's family suggested a trip to Colorado, we thought it would be fun for the four of us to be reunited again."

"The four of you who are now sitting in this FBI office."

"Yep. Ryan and I, Sophie and Jake." Her hand smacked the table. "Hey, you probably know Jake. Jake Taylor—the snowboarder. He's a silver medalist."

Years of training let Agent Martinez retain his stony outward appearance, but internally, he cringed at that news. This afternoon just kept getting better and better. He hadn't realized Jake Taylor was one of the teens. That made things infinitely more difficult.

The star athlete had a certain knack for being in the news. Martinez needed to speed things along before the press somehow found out Taylor was sitting in one of his interrogation rooms—otherwise, he didn't stand a chance of getting to the cabin tonight. The salacious news of Jake Taylor being questioned at an FBI field office would, without a doubt, be the lead story of every weekend broadcast, further complicating Martinez's life and completely ruining his weekend.

"Okay. Well, Josie, let's get right to it. Why don't you start at the beginning and tell me about this week?"

Josie folded her legs into a pretzel shape, making herself "comfortable" on the hard chair.

Part 1
Josie

THE AIRPLANE DESCENDS toward the flat, dusty plains. I've never been to Colorado but honestly, I expected something a bit more spectacular. Where are the famous Rocky Mountains I've heard so much about? All I see out my window are shades of brown— a stark contrast from the green lushness we left behind in Minnesota. So far, this state is not living up to its Colorful Colorado slogan. I turn toward a much better view...my sweet, handsome boyfriend, Ryan.

"Thanks again for bringing me along on this trip."

His fingers lace between mine. "Did I have a choice? You'd never let me live it down if I came to visit Sophie without you."

Earlier this summer, I spent a week working at a camp for disadvantaged teens with Ryan, his cousin Sophie, and her boyfriend Jake. The four of us had an amazing time. Beforehand, I'd been so worried about helping out there and about meeting Ryan's favorite cousin. Then I found out Sophie's boyfriend was a famous snowboarder and...well, it was all a little overwhelming. But the week had been great. And now, I can't wait to see them again.

I squeeze Ryan's hand. "You're right. I definitely would've made the rest of your summer miserable if you'd left me behind."

He opens his mouth to respond but his little sister, Annabelle, leans across him from the aisle seat. Her big brown eyes fix on me.

"Josie, you're going to love Colorado. Since Ryan wouldn't let me sit next to you on the plane, can we sit together on the way up to the dude ranch?"

"Sure." I adore Annabelle. She's about the same age as my little brother, but way cuter. Why couldn't I get a sibling of the non-annoying type?

Her freckled face beams. "I could try and braid your hair again."

"That would be fantastic."

Ryan's eyebrows rise. He's probably remembering the last time Annabelle tried braiding my hair. Smoothing out all those knots took an abundance of patience.

"I'm gonna have to veto that idea." Ryan comes to my hair's rescue. "Remember how curvy the road gets up through the mountains? You don't want to get carsick."

Her face sags in disappointment. "But when we get there, you and Josie will run off with Sophie and her boyfriend."

Ryan nods. "Probably, but you'll have Sam to play with. And I'm sure Grandpa will keep you entertained."

"I guess." Her shoulders fall with the weight of the world.

"Maybe we can play a car game on the drive up." I hate seeing her sweet face lined with disappointment.

She brightens a little. "Okay."

Three hours of various car games later, we pull off the main highway, which led us up into the beautiful rugged Rockies. This part of the state is much more picturesque. I'm starting to understand all the hype.

Ryan's dad navigates a few dirt roads to the welcoming arched gate of the Double L Dude Ranch. After another half mile of unpaved road, we spot the ranch buildings, all made from massively thick logs. Horses graze peacefully out in a pasture. Picture perfect.

We park between a Jeep and an oversized pickup in front of the main lodge. A young boy, around Annabelle's age—about ten or so—flies out of the lodge and sprints toward us. Annabelle squeals and jumps out of the car.

"Let me guess...Sophie's brother?"

Ryan pulls on the door handle. "Yep, that's Sam."

As the rest of us exit the vehicle, Sophie, Jake and three adults join us. While the relatives greet each other with hugs, I head straight to Jake and throw my arms around him.

"Ahh...." He tentatively pats my back. "Hi, Josie, good to see you again."

I pull away and smile at him. "Sorry, I just got caught up in the moment."

But as soon as I release him, Annabelle wraps her arms around him as well. "Hi, Jake, I'm Annabelle."

"Hey, nice to meet you." Her hug is returned with a shoulder squeeze, as opposed to the flinch and awkward tap I received.

I decide not to be offended. I'm aware that he prefers interacting with his pint-sized fans.

Annabelle pulls away and stares up at him, the way the rest of us wish we could—with complete awe and devotion softening her face. Not staring at the gorgeous snowboarder takes an abundance of self-control. "I'm such a *huge* fan!"

You and me both, girlfriend.

"Thanks, so much. I've heard a lot about you from Sam."

Annabelle doesn't answer but continues to stare at him, her expression dripping admiration. Jake's finally rescued from Annabelle's adoration when Ryan comes to greet him. While they do some handshake/bro hug thing, Sophie and I embrace.

With all the hugs out of the way, Ryan introduces me to the others. "Josie, this is my Aunt Valerie and Uncle Dave."

"Okay, let me get this straight," I say to Sophie's mom. "You and Ryan's dad are brother and sister?"

She smiles. "Yep. I've had to put up with him for my entire life." Ryan's dad responds with a wink. She turns back to me. "We're glad you and Jake could join our family vacation. We've heard a lot about you. Sophie told us that you're an actress and have a beautiful voice."

"Oh, well, musical theater's kinda my thing. Anyway, thank you for letting us be a part of your family trip. The four of us had so much fun when we met earlier this summer." I turn to the elderly gentleman I hadn't met yet. But no introductions are necessary. It's like looking into the future. This is what my handsome boyfriend will look like in about sixty years. "You must be Grandpa Frank."

"Guilty." He reaches out his hand, but I move in for the hug. A waft of Old Spice, coffee, and rugged outdoorsy-ness greets me.

"I understand it was your idea to get the family together this summer. So I should be thanking you for letting Jake and I tag along."

He chuckles. "The more the merrier. Maybe you two can keep Ryan and Sophie out of trouble."

A burst of laughter erupts from the parents.

"It's far more likely they'll add to the trouble," Ryan's dad says.

That's not out of the realm of possibility.

I turn back to Grandpa Frank. "I hear you were an Air Force pilot."

"Yes, ma'am." He salutes me.

"I don't know if Ryan told you, but I spent last year collecting veterans' stories for a book that my mom and I are collaborating on together. She's an author and this is our first joint project." Better than the usual middle-grade books that include my mishaps. "Anyway, I can't wait to hear about some of your adventures."

"It would be my pleasure. But I'm not sure I have anything interesting to share."

"Knowing your son and grandson and their mischievous ways, I'd bet that's not true."

He grins the same McNaulty grin that Ryan and his dad share. That and the sparkle in his eyes prove my point.

As Sophie's dad pulls the last of our luggage from the rented SUV, another couple joins us. They're probably a few years older than the parents. A black and white dog with a red bandana around its neck trots behind them. Gray hair peeks out from under the tall, lanky gentleman's cowboy hat which shadows bushy eyebrows and moustache, and tanned skin that matches the aged leather of his cowboy boots. His wife's dishwater blond hair is pulled back in a ponytail. She wears a plaid shirt tucked into her jeans. The red bandana under the collar of her shirt is a perfect match to the dog's.

"Hi!" She offers her hand to Ryan, and then to me, her smile warm and welcoming. "Welcome to Double L Ranch. We're the Jamesons." She jerks her head toward her husband. "This is Lee and I'm Lola."

Ryan shakes Lee's hand. "Lee and Lola, the double L's."

"Yep. That would be us." Lola provides the cheery response, while her husband gives a curt nod.

I'm instantly comfortable with these two. She seems like a cross between a sweet, doting grandmother and a feisty Annie Oakley. He exudes a quiet strength that only a rugged cowboy could possess. If I were a cow I'd follow him anywhere.

I smile at Lola. "I love your name." Unable to stop myself, I proceed to sing part of a song from one of my favorite musicals—"*Whatever Lola Wants, Lola gets.*"

Lee's bristly eyebrows furrow as he stares at me. Lola's brown eyes widen.

I glance at all the eyes focused on me. "Haven't any of you ever seen *Damn Yankees*?"

"'Fraid not." I finally get to hear Lee's deep, gravelly voice. "But the lyrics fit my wife well. We'll make it her theme song."

Lola elbows her husband. "Josie, you have a beautiful voice! I'll have to tell Vinnie. He usually starts singing cowboy songs around the campfire after supper. Maybe you can join him." She wraps her arm around her husband's. "Well, it's such a pleasure to meet you. I hope you all have a wonderful week. I'll let the others show you around."

As a group, we trudge around the main lodge. Noticing all the reddish dirt everywhere, I'm guessing neither my white sneakers nor my adorably cute pastel shorts will be very practical here. It had been hard, packing for a dude ranch vacay. What did one wear? Ryan thought I was over-analyzing the situation, but the right outfit is always a plus.

Behind the main lodge, a fenced-in area contains a swimming pool and a playground. Lining the recreation area are small cabins, five on each side.

"We have all the cabins on the west side," Sophie's mom explains. "Dave, Sam and I are in the first cabin. Sophie and Josie, you'll be in the second one. Jake and Ryan have the middle cabin. Rick, Celeste, and Annabelle are in the next one. And Dad has the last cabin."

I lean into Grandpa Frank. "I'm glad you're on the end. You can protect us from any wild animals."

He winks. "Will do."

I follow Sophie into our tiny cabin. There's one main room, furnished with a couch, two chairs and a coffee table. Scenic paintings and old tools decorate the walls. Two open doors reveal the smallest bathroom I've ever seen, along with a bedroom offering two bunkbeds covered in pretty patchwork quilts. Sophie's bags are already spread out on one of the beds. I toss my stuff on the other.

When we rejoin the group, everyone is giving Ryan's dad a hard time about the brown leather cowboy hat he's wearing.

"Hey, we're on a dude ranch, it's important to look the part." He glances at me, his eyes pleading for assurance. "Right, Josie?"

The new role he's trying to pull off is far from convincing. I mean, seriously—his name-brand running shoes don't exactly scream cowboy. Still, I want to help the guy out. "Absolutely. When you're playing a character, the smallest details are extremely important."

He pulls the rim of the hat lower. "Told you so. Now, let's mosey on and take a gander at this little ol' ranch."

Ryan leans toward me. "You shouldn't encourage him."

The rest of the tour includes an archery area, outdoor grills and tables, a large barn with stalls full of beautiful horses, and a corral just outside the big doors. Finally, we end up back at the main lodge.

Our little posse is barely through the door when Ryan and Jake spot the ping pong table and rush toward it. Let the competition begin. These two can't help but compete—at everything. Sam and Annabelle become their enthusiastic

13

cheering squad. Sophie and I exchange mutually exasperated glances.

A large fireplace circled with couches anchors the middle of the room. The ping pong table and an activity counter are on the right while a dining area takes up the left side of the space.

I pick up one of the brochures from the counter, checking out all the available activities. "This is going to be a great week. Look at all the fun stuff we can do." I turn to Sophie. "Did you bring your camera?"

She looks at me with an "are-you-serious" tilt of the head.

Silly question. I learned earlier this summer that Sophie's camera is like an Amex card, she never leaves home without it.

Sophie's mom comes up behind us. "There's a special chuckwagon dinner tonight around the campfire. You kids have a couple hours if you want to do some exploring beforehand."

Perfect. "Thanks, Mrs. Metcalf, I'd love that. I've never been to Colorado before."

"I have just the activity." Sophie glances at the boys, who are walloping the ping pong ball at each other. "Think we can tear them away from their game?"

We approach cautiously as the white ball zings back and forth across the table.

Sophie speaks. Brave girl. "I hate to break up this little duel of yours, but we have a few hours until dinner. Why don't we check out that four-wheeling trail Mr. Jameson suggested?"

"Four-wheeling?" Not exactly sure what that means.

"Hold on," Jake answers. "I'm about to be crowned champion."

"In your dreams," Ryan snaps back.

Sophie looks at me with a roll of her eyes. "What are the chances that whoever loses will demand they play best two out of three?"

"Pretty darn high, I'd guess." Almost a guarantee with these two.

She nods then turns back to the boys. Her face scrunches up and I know she's wondering how to end this match before we're stuck here watching them all afternoon. An idea percolates in my mind and I move toward the table. Jake slams the ball with his paddle, and I snag it out of the air before Ryan can return the shot. But instead of gracefully catching the ball like I'd visualized, it bounces off my wrist and ricochets into my forehead.

"Oww!" My fingers cover the tender spot.

Ryan lays down the paddle and comes over to me. "You okay?" He pulls my hand from my head, takes a look at my forehead and winces.

"That bad?"

"No, not at all—as long as you were hoping for a giant lump on your forehead."

Oh, great. What was I thinking? That's easy to answer. I wasn't – as usual.

"Does it hurt?" Sophie comes closer to check out the damage.

"No. It's fine. At least I successfully stopped their game."

"Well, good job," she says.

"She looks like a cyclops!" Sam yells.

"Sam!" Sophie shoots her brother a murderous look. He flinches. My cheeks burn.

"But a beautiful cyclops." Ryan grins before leaning in to kiss my newest injury.

15

I glance at Sophie for her opinion.

The look in her eyes contradicts the nod of her head. "It's hardly noticeable but I'll grab you some ice anyway."

"No!" Sam yells. "I'll get it!" He scurries off toward the kitchen.

Jake runs his hand through his thick dark hair. "Hey, I'm sorry."

I shrug. "No worries, it wasn't your fault." Just me acting before thinking—like always.

Sam returns with the ice. "I'm sorry for what I said. You could never look like a cyclops." He hands the bag to me. "You're too pretty."

I hug him, then reassure them all that I'm fine. Fine, except maybe for my wounded pride. After successfully turning the attention away from my deformed forehead, the four of us leave the lodge to pile into Jake's open-top Jeep.

"Cool ride, dude." Ryan emphasizes his opinion with an admiring whistle.

The vehicle roars to life. "Yeah, it's a nice little perk for being their spokesman."

"Really?" I adjust the ice bag. "The company gave you this?"

Always being recognized might be annoying, but some of the guy's perks are pretty sweet.

Jake shrugs. "Yeah." As we drive out to the main road, leaving a cloud of dust in our wake, he glances at Sophie. "Okay, Bloomers, you're the navigator. Get us to the trail."

"Bloomers?" Ryan leans back. "I've got to hear this story."

Sophie laughs. "Basically, I remind him of a tough, Old West girl."

"Makes sense. Tough is always how I describe you."

Sincerity is lacking from Ryan's words—on purpose, I think.

She tosses her hair over her shoulder. "Hey, I'm not the one who squealed like a girl that time a cute little gecko wandered too close."

"*Wandered* near me? I remember it more like when I innocently reached into my lunch bag and pulled out a lizard." Ryan ignores her giggles. "Did I ever get you back for that one?"

Sophie's head snaps toward him. "Are you kidding? That was payback for you choosing the perfect walking stick for me—the one covered in sticky sap. Which, I might add, is nearly impossible to remove. Everything I touched stuck to me for the rest of the day."

Just thinking of it makes me long for hand sanitizer.

As we pick up speed, Jake manually shifts gears. "You two are dangerous. Hopefully Josie and I can stay out of your crosshairs."

Sophie turns the radio on. Soon we're all lost in our own thoughts, listening to the song and enjoying the scenery. Pines and aspens blur by while my hair whirls around my face. I smooth it as best I can then twist it into a hopefully stylish messy bun.

Eventually we turn off the road onto a narrow, rugged path. We creep along as Jake maneuvers through deep gullies and around large boulders. The beauty of the rocky hill before us looks menacingly steep as he drives towards it. We're going up that? They can't be serious. But, alas, they are. I cling to Ryan's hand as we make our way up the rocky incline, the Jeep pitching back and forth in a terrifying side-to-side cant.

"Umm... are you sure this is a road?" A savage jerk of

the vehicle causes me to bite my tongue. I glance at Ryan, the horror on my face reflecting off his aviator sunglasses.

Sophie smiles at me. "Yep, this is a four-wheeling trail. Not a fan?"

She had subjected herself to this torture more than once?

"No, sure, it's great." My head falls against the head rest as the Jeep's angle dramatically increases. *Please Lord, keep us from tipping backwards.*

"Don't worry, Jake knows what he's doing." Sophie squeezes his shoulder.

I grip Ryan's hand even tighter and notice he's also clinging to his seat. Even Jake's knuckles are white as he holds onto the steering wheel. He expertly swerves around a giant boulder, through a patch of mud, down into a deep gully, then back out again. My brain feels like a boomeranging pinball as we're jostled around. What is wrong with these people? Do they really think this is fun?

I'm still contemplating Jake's and Sophie's sanity as we near the top of the hill. Soon the terrain levels off and Jake stops the Jeep.

Thank you, Lord, for keeping us safe.

Ryan grips the roll bar, stands up, and surveys the surrounding view. "Whoa."

I finally exhale and glance around. *Holy moly.*

The view is unbelievable. A vast mountain range spreads before us. The tops of some of the peaks are still white with snow, even in the middle of summer. The mountains are enormous, towering heavenward against the deep blue sky. No wonder they all laughed when I called the Minnesota landscape "mountainous" earlier this summer.

"This. Is. Stunning." I resist the sudden urge to sing "Climb Every Mountain" from *The Sound of Music.* "I've never seen anything so majestic."

Sophie climbs out, camera in hand, ready to capture the beauty.

Jake hops out then turns toward me. "Worth the ride up?"

"Absolutely." The perilous ordeal flees my mind in an instant. Besides, what's that quote? Whatever doesn't kill you makes you stronger?

He reaches for my hand to assist me out of the Jeep. I'm impressed with his gentlemanly manner, but when my foot touches the ground and my wobbly legs crumble, I realize he had an alternate reason—to keep me from face-planting. Should I be offended that he thinks I'm so clumsy or surprised that he knows me so well? I'll choose option number three, and just go with thankfulness.

Using his hand, I steady myself. "Thanks."

He smiles. "It took Sophie some time to get used to the bumpy rides too."

We wander around, admiring the view from every angle. Eventually, we all end up piled on a large boulder, staring out at the Rockies. The vast wilderness in front of us is like a rolling sea of mountains and trees, stretching out endlessly.

Sophie peers through her camera, focusing her lens. "Hey, there's a campsite down there."

She passes the camera around, so each of us can look through the zoom lens.

"It's like a little village." I survey the four tents surrounding a fire pit. Laundry hangs from tree branches.

"I don't see any roads leading there," Jake says, on his turn to stake out the camp. "They must've hiked in."

"Wow, that's roughing it." I shiver at the thought. No running water? No bathrooms? No electricity?

No, thank you.

When I hand the camera back, Sophie smiles. "This view is really pretty. Let me get a photo of you two."

Ryan wraps his arms around me, and we smile for the camera.

Sophie adjusts the lens and snaps a photo. "That was good, but can you move just a little to the right?"

We shift to the right.

She pulls the camera from her face, her artistic eye not liking what she sees in the viewfinder. "There's a little too much shadow on Ryan's face. Why don't you separate just a bit?"

He unwraps his arms from around me, and we just stand next to each other. This might have to be my new profile pic. As long as the giant lump isn't too obvious.

She nods. "Great. Maybe just one more step to the right."

I shuffle to the right.

"AHH!"

My head snaps toward Ryan. He's now about a foot below me, sprawled out in a bed of pine shrubs. He must have stepped off the edge and fallen into the bushes.

Sophie's laughter sends my focus back to her.

She holds up her camera. "I think I captured every second of that epic fall with my high shutter speed."

Ryan ambles out of the mass of low-growing evergreens. He brushes his hands, keeping his eyes on Sophie. "And so it begins."

Tears of laughter stream down Sophie's cheeks. "Sorry, but the look on your face was priceless."

Jake and I glance at each other, complete understanding communicated with one simple look. We might be in for a long week with these two and their pranks.

"All right." Ryan ignores Sophie's continued fit of

giggles. "Think it's time to head back down?"

She wipes her eyes. "Probably."

Jake grins at me. "If you thought the ride up was fun, you're in for a treat."

"Why?" I ask suspiciously.

Sophie finally composes herself. "You may want to hang on tight to something, so you don't fall out."

"What?" A premonition of doom washes over me.

"Just kidding."

But she really wasn't. The ride down is a new realm on the spectrum of terrifying. The angle is ridiculously steep, like on a rollercoaster when the car trundles slowly up a towering hill, then edges over the top before plummeting straight down, sending everyone's stomach hurtling to their throats. Yep. Pretty much just like that, except we are also jostled around by the uneven ground and there's no track to keep us firmly attached and prevent us from flipping end over end.

One thought keeps repeating itself. How can this be Jake and Sophie's idea of fun? The lack of oxygen at this mile-high altitude must have affected their judgment.

But, somehow, by the time we are safely down and have avoided death, I'm rethinking it all. It hadn't actually been *all* that bad, had it? In fact, I might have even enjoyed it...just a little.

a GENT MARTINEZ STARED at the teen girl in front of him. Her unnecessarily detailed story hadn't explained anything of relevance. And something didn't add up. She wasn't the typical teen he usually dealt with. Her excessive talkativeness was far from the sullen, defiant teen-talk he was used to.

He glanced at his notes. "Can we go back to something you said earlier?"

She twirled a strand of long hair around her finger. "Sure."

"You said you collect and write veterans' stories." Though this completely irrelevant piece of information had no bearing on the case, it was the most interesting thing she'd said. Why would a girl her age waste her time with veterans? "Is that true or did you just say that to get on..." He flipped through his notes. "Grandpa Frank's good side?"

"Of course it's true. My mom's an author and we've been compiling the stories together, getting them ready for publication." Her forehead crinkled. "Why would I make something like that up?"

Why, indeed? Sure seemed like an odd project for a teenage girl to care about. He rolled his wrist to check his watch, and his heart dropped. This was not going as quickly as he'd hoped. He still had three others to question.

Josie stretched her arms over her head. "Are we keeping you from your weekend plans?"

"Yes." He searched through his notes to see if anything else caught his eye.

"Is Mrs. Agent Martinez waiting for you?"

He glanced up. Deciding her question was probably innocent, he answered. "No. Just my fishing cabin and the solitude of my usual weekend."

She leaned forward. "That's seriously what you do every weekend?"

He confirmed with a nod.

"I guess it would be peaceful, but doesn't it get a little lonely?"

"I deal with people all week. I'm ready to be alone once the weekend hits."

"Really? No friends or family? Completely alone?"

This girl was nothing if not persistent. "Let's get back to the issue at hand. Everything you told me was all very interesting and I'm sure it's leading to something. Was that the night you first ran into our suspects?"

She shook her head. "No. First Jake and Ryan accidentally shot a man."

That got his attention. "Excuse me?" She could have led with that info.

"Well, I should clarify. They *almost* shot a man."

He sat up straighter. "With a gun?" Was there more to this case than he realized?

Her whole body flinched. "A *gun*? No. Where would you get that impression?" She stared at him as if she'd never heard of a gun before.

"In my line of work, that is usually the first thing that comes to mind when someone talks about a shooting."

"Oh. That makes sense. But no, this was with arrows."

He pinched the bridge of his nose. "They shot—oh,

excuse me—they *almost* shot someone with arrows?"

"Exactly!" She flashed him a smile.

"Do you mind explaining?"

"Oh, sure. The next morning, we decided to check out the archery range on the property before going off on another excursion."

Agent Martinez rubbed his forehead. "Go on."

"The four of us were all minding our own business, shooting arrows at the targets. Well, actually, those three were all doing great. I kept snapping my arm in the string." She rubbed her forearm. "Let me tell you, that really hurts. I had a welt for a few days."

Agent Martinez leaned his head against his hand. "To match the welt on your forehead?"

The teen smiled. "Luckily that forehead one didn't last long. By the time we got back from our four-wheeling ride, it was gone."

He shut his eyes. What had he done to deserve this punishing case? "Thank goodness. You were telling me how Jake and Ryan shot someone."

"Right. Ryan was trying to show me how to shoot properly, but I eventually gave up. And as it always goes with Jake and Ryan, they began competing—seeing who could get the closest to the bullseye. When that didn't determine a winner, they had this bad idea to shoot toward each other's targets from where they stood. But they both missed what they were aiming for. The arrows went between the targets, and someone started yelling."

She paused for a moment, her eyes flicking to Agent Martinez. "That's not like a crime or anything, is it?"

"No."

She nodded, then happily continued. "We were all scared

that they'd actually hit someone, so we ran to the woods in the direction of—well, some pretty angry obscenities. A man was back there, pulling an arrow out of a tree trunk. He glared at us while we apologized. He was super grumpy, but really, who could blame him? I'm sure I'd be a little salty if I'd almost been shot by an arrow. But when he got in our faces with his string of curses, Sophie pointed out that he was on private property. That cooled his attitude."

Agent Martinez sat up in his chair. Maybe she would provide some useful intel after all. "Who was this guy?"

"Precisely! That's what I was wondering because he did not look like he was one of the ranch hands. He was wearing work boots instead of cowboy boots, a heavy-metal band t-shirt and this greasy baseball hat over his long blond hair. Oh, and he had this massive tattoo of a snake on his bicep. Well, when Sophie implied that he was trespassing, he shoved the arrows back to us and walked away. At the moment, we didn't think a lot about it. We were just thankful that we hadn't speared someone. It wasn't until later that we started wondering more about him."

Agent Martinez made his way to the break room, in desperate need of another dose of caffeine. He glanced at his watch and groaned. So much for getting out of here in time to head to the lake while it was still light out. Josie had been more than willing to talk...and talk...and talk—but she'd provided no useful information.

With his mug re-filled with fortifying, strong black coffee, he headed back down the hall. He glanced between the four doors of the interrogation rooms. Maybe it was time to try one of the other kids. He opened the nearest door.

A young man sat at the familiar metal table, leaning back

in his chair. His bold glare and crossed arms conveyed his annoyance.

"Hi, Ryan, I'm Agent Martinez. I'd like to ask you a few questions."

"Sure."

"I just had a chat with Josie. She's your girlfriend?"

Beneath a fall of light brown hair, intense green eyes held his gaze. "Yep."

Agent Martinez set his mug on the table then sat in the chair across from Ryan. "I appreciate you kids coming in to help unravel this story."

Ryan's jaw twitched. "Did we have a choice?"

"Probably not."

"We didn't do anything wrong. Is this whole interrogation thing necessary?"

"I just need to take your statements, then you can be on your way."

We all can. This kid's hostility was going to make Martinez's task difficult. He needed to defuse the situation if he wanted answers. Maybe Josie had a point—making people feel more welcome might be a good idea.

"Josie and I had a nice little chat. She's quite unique, isn't she?"

The corner of Ryan's mouth twitched then turned up into a lopsided grin.

Finally, a relaxed reaction. The agent leaned back in his chair. "She's got a lot of spunk."

Ryan nodded. "Yeah. People don't always know what to think of her. She's got this zest for life, but it sometimes causes fluke accidents, since she tends to leap before she looks."

This was working. Ryan was beginning to relax. "She

27

told me a bit about you and Jake Taylor and your competitive streaks."

Ryan smirked. "Yeah, don't know why, but we can't seem to stop competing. We're both competitive guys and have fun with it."

Agent Martinez nodded. "I've followed Jake's story over the years. Actually, the best piece I ever read about him was written by your cousin Sophie. He always came across as a spoiled hot-head to me until I read Sophie's article. Seeing how his instant fame affected him and his friendships was eye-opening. He probably doesn't have many friends to just hang out with and be a teen."

"Yeah, I guess." Ryan's shoulders relaxed.

The change in the young man's demeanor told Martinez he'd succeeded in creating a rapport. Hopefully the boy would stop being defensive and be more open to talking now.

The agent opened his notebook. After questioning Ryan about the information Josie gave him and finding their stories matched, Agent Martinez turned his focus to the next part of the story.

"Okay, Josie filled me in up until the archery mishap. Can you tell me what happened next?"

The teen chuckled. Then he glanced at Agent Martinez and stiffened up again, probably remembering he was talking with an FBI agent. "That was totally an accident, and no one was hurt."

"I understand. I'm just trying to establish a timeline. What happened next?"

Ryan studied his hands. "Well, let's see. That was Tuesday morning. Not much else happened that day. We all drove to Aspen to see the town and the ski resort. Jake showed us where he'd competed on the halfpipe during the Mountain Madness Games. The entire family decided to ride the lift chair up the mountain. Everyone else wanted to explore and hike around the top, but the four of us rented mountain bikes to ride down the mountain. Unfortunately, a few minutes into the ride, Josie somehow got her shoelace caught in the bike chain, busting the chain and her shoe."

The agent's eyebrows raised. That girl was a walking mishap.

Ryan shrugged. "These things have a way of happening to Josie. As I said, she acts before she thinks, making for some interesting situations."

The agent clamped his lips shut to keep his stony expression.

"So," Ryan continued. "The girls ended up walking their bikes down while Jake and I raced." He eyed the recorder. "And for the record, I beat him down."

Agent Martinez nodded. "Duly noted. Now, can we get back to the matter at hand?"

"Oh, sure." Ryan shifted in his chair. "I guess the best place to start would be Wednesday morning."

Part 2
Ryan

$\mathcal{I}$ 'M PULLED OUT of a dream that I think was really great, but now I'll never know because of a pounding on the door. I force an eyelid open to check the ceiling, where the time is projected from my nightstand clock. The red glowing numbers are not there—just the ceiling, which is only a foot from my face. A tsunami of claustrophobia hits me. Where am I? I glance around the room.

To my left, Jake is sprawled across a bunk bed. Ah. Family vacation. Private cabin.

He looks at me through one half-opened eye. "Race you to the door."

I sink into my pillow. "Nice try. You go ahead. I'll let you win this one."

"Rock, paper, scissors?"

"All right," I sigh. But the incessant pounding ceases.

"Breakfast is in ten minutes!" Sam screams.

Jake and I eye each other again and suddenly spring out of bed, each of us trying to be the first to hit the shower.

Breakfast consists of eggs, pancakes, and a variety of meats. Jake and I probably each devour an entire pig, with all the bacon and sausage we scarf down. When the plates are cleared and the tables washed, we discuss the plans for the day.

"I was thinking it would be fun to go fishing." Grandpa sips his third cup of coffee.

"Yes!" Sam bellows.

Fishing? I could be down with that. I feel that competitive twitch in my core. As a born-and-raised resident from the Land of 10,000 Lakes, I should have a distinct advantage over Jake.

I lean toward him. "I bet I can catch more fish than you."

He nods, a dare in his eyes. "You're on. And since you got to shower first this morning, I get to choose a punishment for the loser." He leans closer. "Cleaning all the fish."

I ignore the roll of Sophie's eyes. "Hope you like fish guts."

"I bet you both that I catch more than either of you," Sophie states.

"That would mean you'd have to put down your camera and pick up the fishing pole."

The glint in her eye means I'm in trouble. She'll stay out all day if she has to, just to prove me wrong. But that's okay. As long as I beat Jake, who cares?

Lola pours the last of the coffee into Grandpa's mug. "Sounds fun. We'll cook up all the trout you bring home."

Dad stands and stretches, then places that ridiculous cowboy hat on his head. The urban cowboy look is almost as bad as when he tried to fit in with the Harley riders at Sturgis. "Hope you have a backup plan for dinner. Sam and Annabelle will probably scare all the fish away, skipping rocks across the lake."

Lola laughs. "Don't worry, you'll never starve around here. I'll round up enough fishing poles and bait for all of you."

"I haven't fished in a long time, but it sounds fun," Josie says. "But I'm not real fond of putting the worms on the hook." She wraps her arms around my bicep and leans her head on my shoulder, her eyelashes fluttering. "Will you do it for me?"

Sam blurts out an answer before I can say a thing. "I'll help you, Josie! I'll be your personal assistant!"

"Oh, Sam. That's so sweet. Thank you." Josie reaches out and touches his arm.

"Watch out, Ryan," Sophie loudly whispers. "I think you've got competition for Josie's affections."

I grin. The kid's got game. "Hmm. I'll have to keep my eye on him."

Annabelle squeezes herself between Jake and Sophie. Pure adoration transforms her face as she gazes at the sports superstar. *Good grief.*

"If Sam's helping Josie, can Jake help me?"

"Nope," Grandpa states. "I'm teaching you and Sam all the tricks of the trade today."

Dad adjusts the brim of his new accessory. "More like, he's corrupting the younger two like he did the older ones."

The four adults look between Sophie and me.

"Who...us?" Sophie innocently asks.

I nod in agreement. "What've we ever done?"

My mom turns to Josie. "As I'm sure you know, these two are always causing mischief for one another."

She smiles conspiratorially. "Yeah, I've noticed."

Aunt Valerie tilts her head toward her father. "What you may not know is that their grandpa always encouraged it."

"The original instigator of the shenanigans," Uncle Dave adds.

Josie leans into Grandpa, resting her head on his shoulder. "Grandpa Frank the trouble-maker—who knew?"

Before Grandpa can clear his good name, the doors of the lodge swing open and Lee saunters in to join us at our table.

"Mornin', folks."

"Been rustlin' up the cows already this morning?" Dad asks.

"Do you even know what rustlin' means?" Aunt Valerie throws her napkin at him. Doesn't matter the age—siblings enjoy ragging on each other.

He dodges out of the way. "Not exactly. Do you?"

"Doesn't matter. I wouldn't try to use it in a sentence."

Lee shakes his head. "City folk."

Lola hands him a mug of coffee. "Hon, can I get you anything? The boys ate most of the food, but I could probably scrounge up something for you."

"No, thanks. Hey, I just spoke to Charlie. Seems one of their calves is missing."

"Really? How'd that happen?" Lola looks around at our bewildered faces. "Charlie is our neighbor to the north."

"Do you think a wild animal got the calf?" Josie scooches closer to me as if said wild animal might be lurking in the lodge and I need to protect her from it.

Lee sets down his mug. "No. Charlie found some footprints. He thinks someone stole it. Although he tends to be a conspiracy theorist."

Lola rests her hand on her husband's shoulder. "Although that is the second ranch in the area to lose a calf in recent weeks."

Lee nods then clears his throat. "So, what're you folks doing today?"

"Fishing!" Sam hollers.

That kid has only one volume—extreme.

Grandpa stands up. "Enough lollygagging around. Let's go before the fish all disappear."

While Grandpa stands patiently waiting by the cars, Jake

and I load up the fishing gear. Sam and Annabelle make their final trips to the restroom. The girls head to their cabin. Sophie needs her camera and Josie must change into the perfect fishing outfit. Both moms have disappeared into the kitchen to pack a lunch. Dad fails to entertain Lee with a cowboy joke while Uncle Dave sips at the last of his coffee. We should've started this process about an hour ago.

Finally, we are all organized and ready to caravan to the lake. The four of us take the tail position in Jake's Jeep. Near the lake we park along a dirt road and begin to unload all the gear. At least Jake and I are unloading. Josie and Sophie stand gaping at the lake.

"Hey ladies, we could use some help." I gather our fishing poles and the tackle box.

"Yeah, you have all day to take in the scenery." Jake pulls out a cooler.

Josie glances over her shoulder at us. "Haven't you ever heard the saying 'stop and smell the roses'? Look at this place—it's spectacular."

"Stunning." Sophie adjusts her camera lens, and I know she's a lost cause. She'll be snapping photos for the rest of the day.

The girls are not wrong. The deep blue water of the lake surrounded by green aspen trees and pines makes an amazing setting. To make it even more breathtaking, mountain peaks soar up to the cloudless blue sky, leaving their reflection behind in the lake's smooth surface.

But hey, the fish are waiting, and I need to catch more than Jake.

Soon, the whole clan is situated along the bank. The four of us chose our own spot a short way from the others. Sophie and I know from experience that it's best to keep our distance from Sam and Annabelle if we want to catch anything. Surprisingly, throwing rocks, splashing in the water, and yelling don't attract a lot of trout. We're probably still not far enough away from their chaos, but the parents wouldn't be too happy if we completely ditch them all.

While I start putting the fishing poles together, Jake picks out some lures and hooks from the tackle box. Sophie continues to snap photos.

Josie sinks down to sit next to me. "What did you guys think about what Lee said at breakfast—that one of the neighbor's calves was stolen?"

"Yeah, that's too bad." I hand Jake a pole.

Sophie moves a little closer. "I'm glad you mentioned that, Josie. I almost forgot about it. You know, I think the ranch they were talking about is the one adjacent to the archery area."

Jake looks up from his task of attaching bait to the fishing pole. "You think that guy we nearly punctured had something to do with the missing calf?"

Josie reaches for a stick and draws a heart in the dirt. "That's exactly what I was thinking. I mean, there aren't a lot of reasons for anyone to be wandering through a ranch in the middle of nowhere. And he didn't look like a ranch hand."

"We'd better tell Lee and Lola about it when we get back." I hand Josie one of the poles. She takes it to Jake, so he can attach the bait.

Sophie places her camera in its case then wipes her hand on her jean shorts.

"Here, Soph." I hand her a pole.

"Thanks."

Jake baits her hook, then she wanders to the shore.

I set down my pole to watch her cast out her line.

She lifts the fishing pole over her shoulder then thrusts her arms toward the water. The thin fishing line should reel out, and the weighted hook should sail through the air until it plops into the water. But when Sophie casts out, the pole comes apart and the pieces drop into the lake.

Perfection.

"What?" Sophie yelps. She scurries into the water to retrieve the pieces before they sink. "Oh, my gosh! It's so cold!" She hand-fishes all the parts out of the lake, then splashes back to shore.

That was too easy. Like swinging at a low-flying curve ball.

Her eyes catch mine.

I fight to keep a straight face but fail miserably. "Trouble?"

Her eyes narrow into that penetrating glare that always turns my blood to ice.

I smile sweetly. "I'd be happy to give you a refresher course."

"Very funny." Sarcasm drips like the water from her shirt. She plops the broken pole next to me, then moves behind me to wring out the hem of her wet shirt. Cold-water trickles down my back.

"Thanks. It was getting a little warm sitting here."

"How'd you rig that, oh evil one?"

"When I was putting it together, I noticed it was cracked." I hand her my pole. "Here, you can have mine."

"Uh...no thanks. I'll put my own together this time."

I shrug and give her my most innocent look. "Okay, just trying to help."

"Do we have to separate you two?" Josie asks.

"No. We'll behave." I grab my pole and stand up. "Okay, Jake, ready to see how many fish we can catch?"

"Sure. The sooner we catch 'em, the sooner you can start cleaning them."

Only a few minutes after we cast our lines, Sophie's pole starts to twitch.

"Ha! Told you I was a better fisherman than you two." A satisfied smirk plasters on her face.

She reels in her line, nice and slow. As the fish nears the shore, it splashes and flops around trying to escape. "Jake, can you get the net?"

Josie springs up. "I'll get it!" She grabs the net near the tackle box.

"Are you sure?" Her tendency to act before she thinks does not fill me with confidence. "Do you want some help?"

"No, I've got this." She steps on to the rocks and lowers the net into the lake. I watch her try to swoop in under the squirming fish.

"Be careful, the rocks are –"

SPLASH!!

"Slippery."

One moment she's crouching near the fish. The next, she's sitting in the water giving a great impression of a startled emoticon.

I scurry over to help, but before I get there she smiles and lifts up the net with the flailing fish. Her eyes light up in triumph.

"Got it!"

"Way to go!" I reach out my hand to her.

"And you thought I couldn't do it." She grasps my hand and carefully stands. Cold lake water drips from her clothes, and little rivulets trickle down her legs.

I pull her close. "I should never have doubted you. But you know, there are ways to do it without getting drenched."

Sophie holds up her hand towards Josie for a high-five. "Teamwork!"

"Girl power!"

"Hey, what's the commotion over here?" Grandpa saunters over. "Are you guys the first to catch one?"

"Let's be clear," Sophie boasts. "*I* was the first to catch one."

He smiles. "I taught you well, young apprentice." His focus shifts to Josie. "Why are you all wet?"

Josie holds up the net showing off the fish.

"Josie was demonstrating her unique fishing technique," Jake explains.

"It's surprisingly effective, with the added benefit of keeping you nice and cool," I add.

Grandpa adjusts his fishing cap and gives her an appreciative nod.

Yet another of the McNaulty men have fallen powerless to my girl's unique charms.

A few hours later the four of us are strolling through Carbondale in search of an ice-cream shop. The girls have declared our fishing excursion over—they've had enough fishing for one day. Not sure how that is even possible.

"I would've caught more fish if the girls hadn't insisted on leaving," I inform Jake as we make our way down the sidewalk in the small mountain town.

He pats me on the back. "Keep telling yourself that if it makes you feel better."

"Technically, you had more fishing time. I had to help Josie untangle her line—twice—*and* remove the old shoe that she caught."

Jake shrugs. "Make as many excuses as you want, but I caught more fish than you, and that was the bet."

Nailed me on that one.

Sophie pushes past us both. "I'd like to point out who actually caught the most fish."

"You're like a fish whisperer." Josie tells her. "They were just drawn to your line."

Jake pulls opens the door to the ice-cream parlor and holds it while we pile into the little shop. "Sorry, Soph, your big accomplishment doesn't count. I caught more fish than Ryan. Although, somehow he got out of gutting them all."

I pull off my sunglasses. "Is it my fault Sam and Annabelle wanted to master the skill of cleaning a fish?"

Sophie parks both hands on her hips and narrows her eyes at me. "You didn't happen to pay them to help, did you?"

I hold up my hands. "I plead the fifth."

The two teen girls in front of us at the counter turn around, ice cream cones in hand. One of the girls smiles as her gaze slides over our group. Then she sees Jake. Her eyes and mouth widen, making her look a little like the trout we'd just caught. She walks past us, focused only on Jake's face, and trips over her friend's foot. Jake reaches out to keep her from falling, but her ice cream is not as lucky and plops to the floor.

The rest of us look down at the splattered, chocolatey mess but she doesn't seem to notice.

"Oh, my gosh! You're Jake Taylor, aren't you?"

Jake glances at Sophie then back at the girl. "Guilty."

She keeps staring at him, apparently forgetting the rest of us are even there.

"I can't believe this. I'm such a fan! Your picture—it's

in my bed." Blushing furiously, she shakes her head. "I mean in my room. I have a poster of you hanging next to my bed." The way she looks at him, like she's hypnotized, is creepy personified.

I glance at my cousin, who's bottom lip is held tight between her teeth. Does this happen a lot when they're out in public? How does she not get sick of it? Sophie answers my silent query with a roll of her eyes.

Jake smiles politely. "Thanks, that's nice of you to say."

I move closer, tired of this exchange for Sophie's sake. "I think you dropped something."

The girl's mesmerized gaze finally leaves Jake's face and travels to the floor. "Oh. Oops."

Jake glances back at the mess on the floor. "Can we buy you another ice-cream?"

After we order our cones and Jake signs a bunch of autographs, we sit around one of the tables out in front of the store. While Jake and I debate who bore the blame for our fishing lines getting tangled, Sophie points out something across the street to Josie, who turns to us.

"Can you two put away your masculinity for one moment?"

I pull my shoulders back. "No, probably not."

Her elbow jams into my side. "I'm serious. While you two were puffing out your peacock feathers, Sophie and I noticed something."

"What?" Jake licks his ice-cream.

Sophie leans in toward us. "Well, don't make it obvious, but see that restaurant across the street?"

Jake and I turn our heads.

"Seriously?" she snaps. "I said not to make it obvious!

Anyway, see those four men sitting around that table on the patio?"

"Yeah." Four guys having lunch. Who cares?

"I think the one with the green baseball hat is the man from the archery range."

"The one you guys practically shish kabobbed," Josie adds.

Jake squints towards the men again. "Yeah, maybe."

As we watch, trying not to look like we're watching, the four men stand. One of them tosses some bills on the table, then they leave the patio and head down the street, away from us.

"Come on," Josie says. "Let's follow them."

I shake my head. "How do you propose we do that? This isn't exactly a booming metropolis. I think they'll notice."

She pushes away from the table. "Nonsense, there are lots of little stores. We'll window shop."

Sophie pops the last of her cone into her mouth. "I'm game."

Together these girls are trouble—one stubborn and suspicious, the other impulsive and curious. Of the two, neither think through the consequences.

Jakes looks at me. I shrug, so he turns back to them. "Seriously? You think we'll hear them admit to stealing the calf? What good will following them do?"

Sophie shrugs. "I don't know, but look at them. They don't fit in with the whole western ambiance, not even a little."

I glance at the men again. "And we do? They're probably tourists, like us."

"Yeah, but four random men? They're not the same ages. They don't appear to be from the same walks of life." She starts counting off on her fingers. "The one we saw yesterday with the snake tattoo and the long hair looks like a biker. The guy next to him in the oversized plaid shirt is all skin and bones. His clothes are at least three sizes too big. The big husky guy? He's like some rapper, with that shiny gold chain and low-riding jeans. And the other guy's wearing a collared shirt and dress shoes."

She has a point—hard to imagine a more mismatched group than that.

"Plus, they are barely talking to one another," Josie adds. "I agree, something is off. They don't seem like they belong together."

The girls start walking down the sidewalk, pretending to admire items in the windows of the stores. Jake and I are forced to follow along. Through the reflection in the glass storefronts, I notice the men occasionally glance around but they don't seem too concerned with us. They enter the pawn shop on the corner.

We're standing in front of a t-shirt shop. Sophie pulls open the door. "Let's wait in here and see how long they take."

Josie grabs my arm. "A pawn shop seems a little sketchy. Don't you think?"

"You've been watching too many movies. Pawn shops are legitimate businesses." I shake my head. "Besides do you think they're trying to pawn off the neighbor's calf?"

Jake laughs, but the girls ignore us. They also ignore the lady behind the counter who peers at us over the top rim of her glasses like a stern librarian. Eyes focused across the street, the girls sift absently through the stock of t-shirts, waiting for the men to reemerge.

After a few minutes, they do. One of the men pulls a

small yellow box out of a plastic shopping bag. He rips open the packaging, then they pile into an old, beat-up pickup truck and drive away.

"Come on." Sophie marches toward the door.

"Soph!" Desperation edges Jake's voice. "Not everything's a mystery."

"I have to agree." Sure, we've had some adventures, but not every suspicious behavior is criminal.

Sophie shines a bright smile over her shoulder as she exits the store. "I know, I'm just curious."

Josie grabs my hand with steely determination and tugs me along. "Well, we won't know whether or not it's a mystery if we don't investigate."

I give the wary shop owner a polite smile then follow the others out the door.

We cross the street and enter the pawn shop, which seems to be suffering an identity crisis. The store is jam-packed with everything imaginable—guns, jewelry, stereos, furniture. Mass confusion rules the small place. I focus on the sports memorabilia that lines one of the walls. Wonder if they have anything worthwhile.

A man with an extremely shiny bald head stands behind the counter. "Can I help you?"

Sophie approaches. "Hi! You probably get this all the time, but I just love those pawn shop shows on TV and am so curious about them. I mean, that one set in Vegas is just so fun to watch. Anyway, we saw some men leaving and have a bet on what they were pawning off. My friends say some kind of electronics. But I'm guessing it was a piece of jewelry. Like a watch or a diamond ring? Possibly a family heirloom? Or maybe…" She clamps her mouth shut.

Jake shoots me a grin. Sophie really shouldn't have been

the spokesperson—she never has been able to handle her nerves.

Her shoulders rise and fall as she takes a deep breath. "Could you please tell us what they were doing here?"

He cocks his head to the side, his eyes narrowing. "They were actually just browsing. Curious about some of the stereo equipment." A sneer slides across his face as he slowly scans her.

Jake takes a protective step closer. He must have also noticed the guy's predatory vibe… Good.

Josie nudges me. I glance at her then follow her head tilt. She's staring at a display of pay-as-you-go phones. The packaging is bright yellow.

My attention turns back to Sophie, who opens her mouth like she's about to ask the clerk something else.

Jake steps up next to her. "Great. Well, thanks for settling that for us."

He clamps onto her arm and leads her out the door.

Outside the shop, Sophie twists her arm out of Jake's grasp. "Why'd you pull me out of there?"

He glances over his shoulder, as if checking to see if anyone else is around, then walks towards the Jeep. "Because I think you might be on to something."

She hurries to keep up with his long strides. "What? Why?"

He looks back at her. "When you first started asking him questions, before he went into full creeper-mode, beads of sweat gathered above his lip and on his forehead. You made him nervous."

"Oh. I didn't notice. I was too preoccupied with my own nerves. But I did see him shift some papers over whatever he was working on when I approached the counter. And he lied to us. Those men weren't just browsing. We saw the bag—they bought something."

"And we know what that something was," Josie states proudly.

Jake and Sophie both turn towards her. "What?"

"Several disposable phones are missing from the display. And guess what color box they come in?"

Sophie's eyes widen. "Yellow. Why would they need burner phones?"

I try to shake off the disturbing feeling creeping up my spine. "Because they're up to no good."

*a*gent Martinez stared at the teenage boy in front of him. "This would've been a good time to call the sheriff's department."

Ryan tilted his head. "You sure about that? What would they have said when we told them we suspected some guys were up to no good, even though we had no reason to suspect them—well, besides the fact that they bought some disposable phones and dressed funny?"

The agent cleared his throat, conceding the point. He glanced through his notes. Ryan's description of the fishing trip caught his eye. A vivid reminder that his weekend plans were slipping away with each passing moment. But it also brought a wave of nostalgic memories. Something about Ryan's story made him long for the past. He and Maggie used to have so much fun at the cabin. But those times were gone. Now, the cabin was his get-away from the human race. On the other hand, maybe it would be fun to have someone to fish with again.

Ryan shifted in his chair, bringing Agent Martinez back to the present.

"All right. What happened next?"

Ryan grinned. "Let's see. I'd say that's when Sophie fed the ranch dog my dinner."

Agent Martinez closed his eyes. Another non-helpful answer. He didn't get paid enough to have to deal with teenagers. He stood. "I need another cup of coffee."

He trudged down the hall to the breakroom to refill his

mug with strong black coffee. He glanced at the clock on the wall. So much for heading to the cabin tonight. Getting to the bottom of this story was taking forever.

His shoulders sagged as he walked back to the interrogation rooms. He turned toward a third door, ready for a different perspective. He pulled the door open.

Another teen girl sat at the table. Eyes closed, she rubbed her necklace with slender fingers.

"Hi, I'm Agent Martinez."

Her green eyes popped open. The pendant dropped to her chest.

She stood and reached out her hand. "I'm Sophie Metcalf."

She sat, glanced around the room then began to pick at her pink nail polish. "Did you know that the FBI first came to Glenwood Springs because there were so many fugitives hiding out here in the Rockies?" She grimaced. "Of course, you would know that since you're an FBI agent. I just always thought it was kinda interesting." She clamped her mouth shut and stared at him.

He settled into a chair then looked at her. Why was she so anxious? Was she hiding something?

"Sorry." She mumbled. "When I'm nervous, I have a tendency to ramble."

He picked up his notebook. "Why are you nervous?"

"Umm, well, it's not every day I get hauled into an FBI office for questioning."

He flipped through his notes. He felt like he was missing something. It didn't make sense that a bunch of teens on vacation would worry about some rancher's missing calf. Maybe they were more than just witnesses.

"So, I understand you were suspicious of the men you

saw in town and followed them to the pawn shop."

Her long wavy hair bobbed around her face as she nodded.

"Can you explain why you were so interested? I'm sure there must have been more exciting things for you to be doing."

She crinkled her nose. "They seemed to be up to no good."

Then he remembered the article she'd written about Jake. "You aspire to be an investigative reporter, right? Were you hoping to get a story?" Maybe they'd been snooping around where they shouldn't have been.

She shook her head. "No. I didn't actually think about that. I was more concerned about the missing calf."

His eyes narrowed. "Why? Had you ever met that rancher?"

"No, but we felt bad for him and wondered if the man we saw in the archery area had been involved."

He scribbled down her response.

"And of course, Jesus tells us to help one another."

He looked up at her. Was she serious? What teen cared about anyone but themselves, let alone what the Bible said? None he'd met recently.

She tilted her head. "I bet you usually only see bad people in your line of work. But there are a lot of good people out there. Do you have a group of family or friends to help you remember that?"

He shifted in his chair, trying to figure her out. She must've been deflecting attention from herself for some reason. He'd assumed they were witnesses, not suspects, but maybe they were hiding something.

She rubbed her necklace again. For the first time he

noticed the cross she wore around her neck. Could she be genuine?

A smile warmed her face. She let her necklace drop again. "I take it that's a *no*. I hope I'm not being too forward, but church really is a great place to meet nice, supportive people." Her eyes squeezed shut. "Sorry, my nerves always get me talking too much."

He lowered his gaze and flipped to the next page of his notebook. Church? Maggie had liked to go but after she walked out on him and left town, he'd stopped attending. Too hard to face everyone. Some of the folks tried reaching out to him but stopped after their attempts were repeatedly ignored.

He glanced back up to find her watching him. He cleared his throat. *Just focus and get this over with.* "I've had a chance to chat with Ryan and Josie. I was hoping to get your version of events."

She folded her hands and laid them on the table. "Sure."

"Your friends covered the first few days of your vacation—in great detail." A quick rehash of the events with Sophie corroborated Josie and Ryan's version of events. He turned to the last page of his notes from Ryan then rubbed his hand on the stubble that was starting to emerge along his jawline. "Ryan just got done telling me you fed his dinner to the ranch dog."

"What?" Her eyes widened. "He really told you that?" She crossed her arms. "I suppose he neglected to tell you how that *accidentally* happened?"

Agent Martinez leaned back in his chair. Why'd he bring that up? Now he'd have to listen to her side. "Nope. Wasn't privy to that information."

"I didn't mean to dump his dinner, but it served him right.

When we got back from our visit to town, Josie and I went to our cabin to freshen up. Everyone was gathered around the fire when we came out. Some of the ranch hands were working on dinner but had prepared some appetizers for us while we waited. I ate a piece of meat that Ryan offered me. It wasn't until a little while later when I was helping deliver plates of food and was being a really sweet cousin, I might add, by delivering a plate to Ryan, that he told me what the appetizer had been. Apparently, the ranch hands trap animals and cook up the different meats. Well, Ryan informed me that the piece I tried was…" Her face transformed into a look of pure disgust. "Rattlesnake!"

Martinez covered his mouth with his hand, struggling to keep his stony demeanor.

She shuddered. "You have no idea how much I hate snakes. When he told me, my hand automatically shot to my mouth and the plate of trout I was holding dropped to the ground. The dog was on it in seconds."

"You and your cousin have a unique relationship, don't you?"

"Yeah, we kinda like to prank each other." She smirked. "But don't worry, I got him back later." She leaned forward like she was going to share more but bit her lip instead. "Anyway, lucky for him, Josie's sweet. She shared her dinner with him." She paused for another moment then continued talking. "I have to admit, I wasn't sure about Josie when Ryan first introduced us earlier this summer. She's so different from Ryan, being into theater and a bit on the clumsy side. But she grew on me and now we're pretty close. It may seem odd but even though her free spirit gets her into trouble, I can't help but admire her reckless abandon. Sometimes I wish I was less cautious and could just let loose like that." She shifted in her chair. "Sorry, I'm sure you don't want to hear about Ryan and Josie. What can I tell you?"

Agent Martinez took a swig of his coffee, anxious to get on to the important parts of her story. "Why don't you tell me what happened after you saw those men in town."

"Okay, sure."

Part Three
Sophie

*T*HE LOUD, CLANGING bell announcing dinner, gathers all the guests to the outside firepit. The ice cream from earlier is but a distant memory as the incredible aromas make my stomach growl. These cowboys sure know how to cook.

Lola, whose blue bandana tied around her neck matches the camp dog's again, climbs on one of the benches. "We hope you're all having a wonderful time with us this week, enjoying all this beautiful ranch has to offer. The good Lord has truly blessed us with this lovely property. Kindly remove your hats as Lee leads us in a prayer to give thanks for our blessings."

The man of few words removes his cowboy hat and places it over his heart, revealing gray hair plastered to his scalp like a silver swim cap. His deep grumbly voice resonates around the fire. "Dear Lord, thank You for bringing all these lovely folks to our home. We ask that You continue to bless our week with safety, friendship and family. Thank You, Lord, for this meal and the many hands that helped prepare it. In your name, Amen."

I bow my head and make the sign of the cross.

All eyes return to Lola. "To give you a taste of real ranch life, tonight we have prepared a chuckwagon dinner. In true cowboy manner, you will take your plate and walk through the line. We will serve you an authentic meal of beans, barbeque pork, baked potato and roll. Cowboys work hard all day and need a satisfying meal. But for you city folks, we do also serve a salad."

The crowd chuckles.

"We also have cooked up some of the fish the McNaulty clan caught today. Chow time!"

Sam and Annabelle scurry to the front of the line where tin plates are loaded with the tantalizing food. The ranch hands tell jokes as they serve generous portions.

Jake and I sit at a table with Ryan and Josie. Grandpa and one of the ranch hands join us.

"So what're you all doing tomorrow?" The cowboy, who introduced himself as Vinnie, asks.

"We hadn't really thought that far ahead," I answer. "Any suggestions?"

"The rafting is great. Tom's an excellent guide. I could also take you out on the horses sometime."

"Perfect."

Cowboy Vinnie looks at Josie. "Lola tells me you're a singer. Maybe we could sing together one of these evenings."

Her jaw stops moving mid-bite. "Umm. Know any show tunes?"

"Not that I know of. But I think we'll be able to come up with something. Will you sing with me sometime this week?"

She smiles. "Well, if you can miraculously find a song we both know, then sure."

He gives her a curt nod then shovels a spoonful of beans into his mouth.

After dinner, our cowboy friend grabs his guitar and starts strumming. As his deep tenor voice serenades, I curl up in one of the chairs around the fire and watch the dancing flames. Their flickering moves are mesmerizing. Soon Lola and Lee, trailed by the camp dog, bring out items to make s'mores. I study the couple. Should we tell them about the men we've been seeing?

Annabelle skips over to us, interrupting my thought. "Ryan, will you please make me a s'more?"

He stands. "Of course. One of my famous, perfectly toasted masterpieces coming up."

Her sweet smile shines in the firelight. "Thanks. Yours are always the best."

Jake leans forward. "Annabelle, you only think Ryan makes the best because you've never had mine. I'm kinda known in these parts for my s'more-making ability."

Annabelle's doe eyes gaze upon him adoringly. An expression I've become used to when girls look at my boyfriend.

Ryan tilts his head. "Oh, I think I hear a challenge in those words. Annabelle, you've got a huge task on your hand. You're going to need to decide who is the s'more-making king."

Annabelle giggles. Not wanting to be left out, Sam hurries over.

"Can I help judge too?"

I can't stop the eye roll. "Seriously, you two are even competing at s'mores?"

Jake turns to me. "Soph, this is serious business."

As Jake and Ryan work on toasting the perfect marshmallow, Josie decides to show both of them up. She pushes a pillowy-soft marshmallow onto a stick, then holds it near the flames. I watch as it starts to puff up.

"Josie, you're a little close to the flames," Ryan warns her.

"You just worry about your own, I've got this." That's when her marshmallow catches on fire. She tries to blow out the flame but her masterpiece sizzles and pops, transforming into a piece of coal, then as the ashes fall—nothingness. "Oh." She stares at the charred mess at her feet.

Sam jumps to her rescue, taking the stick from her hand. "Don't worry, Josie, I'll make you one."

I've never seen my brother infatuated before—the sincerity in his voice, the sudden gentlemanly manners. Huh…who knew the twerp could be sweet. Maybe there's hope for him after all.

I wake to a clanging sound. Not the welcome jangle of the food bell, but a really loud, annoying metal-on-metal sound. It reminds me of the time Ryan took me to the batting cage and kept smacking the balls with his metal bat.

I roll over to look at Josie. "What is that?"

She props herself up, her long, light brown hair falling into her face. "No clue."

We pull on some clothes and leave our cabin, the sound leading our way like some weird pied piper. As we approach, I have a pretty good idea what it is. Sure enough, we round our cabin and find Jake and Ryan standing next to each other. Ryan tosses a horseshoe across the open space to the pit across from him. The heavy metal arc lands in a cloud of dirt. Jake chuckles at Ryan's miss then throws his horseshoe. It doesn't wrap around the stake either, but lands on top of Ryan's horseshoe with a reverberating clang.

"Don't you two ever give up?" Josie asks as we approach.

The guys turn toward us.

"Morning," Ryan says. Josie launches herself into his arms—a move I've come to refer to as a Josie-jump.

Jake kisses my cheek as I approach. "We had to keep ourselves occupied somehow till our sleeping beauties awoke."

"Next time, find a quieter pastime."

"So, who's winning?" Josie untangles herself from Ryan and perches on a large tree stump.

"Ryan has an unfair advantage." Jake walks toward the far pit for his next turn.

Ryan shakes his head in disagreement. "Throwing a horseshoe is nothing like throwing a baseball."

"Well, it's closer to throwing a baseball than to snowboarding," Jake argues.

Ryan joins Jake at the far pit. "Just admit that I'm better at this event than you are."

"Never." Jake hands Ryan two horseshoes.

I turn to Josie. "This might take all morning and I'm famished. Want to grab some breakfast?"

"Sure, but first, can I try tossing one of those? I've never played this before."

I shrug, and she flounces over to Ryan who hands her one of the horseshoes. I back away, taking cover. Come on, this is Josie throwing a heavy piece of metal in my direction—of course I'm going to be cautious.

Gripping the curve of the horseshoe, she pulls her hand back then swings it forward. Instead of the metal horseshoe sailing to the sandy pit, it flies straight up in the air. Ryan pulls her back as the horseshoe plummets with a thud, inches from where she was standing. Who didn't expect that?

"Oops!" Josie's hand flies to her mouth.

Ryan gives her the sweetest smile, the kind that makes it hard not to say *awww*. "I guess I should've given you a few pointers before letting you loose with a horseshoe."

"Yeah, I don't think this is really my sport." She wipes dusty hands on her shorts.

I love how she's never afraid to at least try new things.

She turns to me. "How about that breakfast, Sophie?"

"Sounds good." I look at the boys. "You guys coming?"

Ryan nods. "We're almost finished. I'm just about to forty points."

"Forty?" I know I shouldn't ask—nothing with these two ever makes sense—but I can't help myself. "Don't we usually play to 21?"

I look at Jake for an explanation, but he's studying the horseshoe in his hand like it's the most fascinating new gadget he's ever seen.

Yeah, something is amiss.

Ryan laughs. "We agreed to end the game when the winner got to twenty-one, but Jake didn't like the outcome, so I suggested we play to thirty. Now, we're up to forty." He turns to Jake. "And that's the final."

Jake shifts his baseball hat, placing it backwards over his dark hair. "The only reason my game is trash is because I'm starving. Why don't we call it a game?"

"Works for me." Ryan pats Jake's shoulder. "Better luck next time."

"Enjoy the glory now—'cause you're going down."

I roll my eyes and walk away. Why had I insisted those two meet?

Their banter continues until we enter the lodge where the rest of the family is gathered. Annabelle and Sam are playing Jenga with Grandpa. As squirmy as Sam is, there's no way that game will last long. We grab some breakfast then settle at the tables with the parents.

"What's on the agenda for today?" Ryan stuffs a forkful

of scrambled eggs into his mouth.

Aunt Celeste sets down her coffee mug. "We were thinking of rafting."

Josie twirls her spoon in her cocoa. "Sounds fun."

My mom nods. "There's a section of the river with very small rapids, which sounds perfect."

Ryan lowers his fork. "Seriously?"

Uncle Rick pats Ryan's shoulder. "That's what you get when you go on vacation with your moms. Safety first."

We're briefly interrupted by a crash of the Jenga pieces.

"I win!" Sam bellows.

"Rematch!" Annabelle crawls around the floor, gathering the fallen pieces.

Lola comes up behind us. "Sawyer—one of the guides we use—could take you kids further down the river. The rapids are a little more intense there."

I can't help but look at Josie. I love the girl, but she really is an accident waiting to happen. "Umm...I'm not sure that's such a great idea."

But Josie, Ryan and Jake think it's a fabulous idea and ignore my concern.

Soon, we're driving to the launch spot on the river where we'll meet the boats and guides. Poor Uncle Rick is forced to leave his precious cowboy hat in the car when we don life jackets and helmets. We get a quick safety lesson, then the five adults and two younger kids pile onto a boat with their guide, Tom. The four of us climb on a raft with Sawyer and two other couples.

Sawyer pushes us away from the shore then hops on as we glide down the smooth-flowing water. I pull out my camera and take some shots of all the contrasting colors. The red rocks, green trees, purple columbines, and blue sky create a stunning palette. Jake shoots me a grin when Sawyer shares some interesting Colorado rafting facts. He loves to tease me about my weird obsession for obscure Colorado history.

I tuck my camera safely away before we reach the small rapids. We carefully listen to Sawyer's instructions and obey when he instructs us to row.

We follow the other raft through the rapids. Annabelle's and Sam's squeals echo around us. Once we're through the section of slightly rougher water, the gentle, flowing current pushes us downriver. After we veer into a side pool and I receive the secret okay from Sawyer, I stealthily move toward the middle of the raft. Ryan suspects nothing…until I push him off the side of the boat.

He falls in, arms flailing. The look on his face is priceless. To make it even better, Jake catches it on his cell phone.

"Refreshing?" I ask when his head pops up.

He splashes water at me. "You're in trouble now, Cous."

I scooch away from the frigid water drops. "You didn't seriously expect me to eat rattlesnake and not pay you back, did you?"

Two strokes through the water and he's to the raft. "Hey, I didn't make you do anything."

Josie reaches her hand out to help him up, not noticing his Wile E. Coyote grin. Nothing good ever comes from that look. It's a clear "beware—danger zone" sign. Before I can warn her, he pulls her in with him.

"AHH! This water is freezing!" She gasps when she manages to catch her breath from the initial shock.

Sawyer laughs. "Considering that yesterday it was snow from on top of the mountain, I'm not surprised."

Annabelle and Sam beg their guide to let them jump in as well, and soon they're splashing around, spraying us all with icy water. Sawyer and Jake add to the chaos as they cannonball into the water, soaking everyone in the process.

Once everyone gets back on board, we drift on down the sparkling river. The sunlight shimmering off the water makes it seem like we're flowing down a pathway of diamonds. After a few more miniature rapids, the guides maneuver the rafts onto a beachy alcove of the river.

"Okay, this is the exit point for raft number one," Sawyer states. "I'm going to help get their raft up to the bus and grab our lunch. The rest of you can explore a little or lay out in the sun and dry off. I'll be back soon. We'll get back on the river in about an hour and hit the larger rapids."

He leaves us to help the other guide. They walk away, with Sam and Annabelle complaining that they can't stay for the larger rapids. The other two couples settle on the rocks to dry off. We pull off our helmets and life jackets.

"There's a path here. You guys want to take a walk?" Ryan holds out his hand to Josie, who is covered in goosebumps.

"Sure." I grab my camera then Jake and I follow.

The path meanders alongside the river.

"This is so beautiful," Josie states between shivers.

"Yeah. Something about mountain streams and rivers is just so peaceful." I snap a few photos of the shimmering water, the rocks and pines adding to the perfect setting. No matter how many photos I take, I'm never quite able to capture the serenity.

As we walk, Josie tells us about a time at Girl Scout camp when she was crossing a rope bridge over a river and somehow lost her footing and fell into the water. "And of course, that little incident made it into my mom's fourth book."

"Must be interesting having a mom who's an author," Jake says.

"Interesting is one word for it. It's actually caused some problems."

I look between the two of them, surprised I never thought of the connection before. "Jake, it's kinda like your life. Neither of you can keep anything private. Because you're famous, all your mistakes become public knowledge—and Josie's are forever set in print."

Josie links her arm through Jake's. "Who knew we had something in common?"

Jake shoots me a look like he's hoping I'll rescue him. I pretend not to notice his silent plea. But he needn't worry, her attachment is short lived. She steps to the side of the path and begins walking along the top of a fallen log. Ryan reaches up to help her balance, but she waves his hand away and does a graceful little pirouette. Her moments of pure elegance are in stark contrast to her penchant for mishaps— a walking enigma.

She leaps off the end of the log. "Oh. I forgot to tell you. Vince and I found some songs we both know. We're going to sing together around the campfire tonight."

"Let me guess." Ryan playfully tugs at her hair. "You convinced him to sing something from a musical about cowboys."

She spins around to look at us, walking backwards. "Don't I wish. I had a great song from *Oklahoma* in mind, but he vetoed it. We're actually singing a few old hymns like *Amazing Grace* and *How Great Thou Art*."

"That sounds good."

Ryan reaches for her arm, expertly guiding her around the tree root in her path. They really are cute together.

"Shh." Jake suddenly stops moving as we come to a denser part of the forest.

"What?" Josie whispers.

"Look." He points through the bushes across the river.

I peek through the shrubs, expecting to see some deer or other wildlife. Instead I spot several men knee deep in the water.

"Are they fishing?" Josie whispers.

Jake shakes his head. "No fishing poles."

Ryan leans over my shoulder. "Hey, aren't those the guys we saw yesterday in town?"

I use my camera to get a closer look, slightly shifting the angle to observe each of the men. "Yep. I recognize that ugly snake tattoo."

"What're they doing?" Jake asks.

I peer at them. "Looks like they're washing up."

"I guess if you're camping, the river would be your only bathtub—a rather cold one." Josie shivers again.

"Yeah, one guy's shaving. Oh. Wait." I adjust the lens to zoom in even closer.

"What?" Ryan asks.

"I think one of them is dying his hair."

"Really?"

"Yeah, there's a box on the rock. And it appears our tattooed friend has cut those long blond locks of his."

Josie grabs my arm. "They're changing their appearance. How weird is that?"

I nod, a shadowy undercurrent flowing through me. "Very." I snap a few photos while we keep our eyes on them.

"Come on." Jake places his hand on my back. "We

should get back to the raft. Sawyer will be waiting for us."

Everyone is caught up in their own thoughts on our silent journey back to the raft. What could those men be up to? Why would they be out here in the wilderness and changing their appearance? And why did they need burner phones? Something is definitely off.

Back at the raft we enjoy a quick lunch then everyone piles on and we head down the river to finish our adventure. By the time we get to the spot where we saw the men, they are gone. I don't have long to contemplate them before we hit the first set of rapids. A narrowing of the river causes the water to rush around large boulders, creating rougher water. Sawyer shouts out commands. Sometimes one side of the boat must paddle, while the other side waits or even back paddles. A few times I'm afraid I'm about to catapult out of the raft. I wedge my feet further under the rubber wall, trying to keep from shooting off my seat into the water.

The river dips down and we go over a small waterfall. Josie screams and the guys laugh. I forget my paddling for a moment and cling onto the handhold. Sheesh! My stomach rolls like I'm on a rollercoaster as we pummel through the water and rocks. I gasp at the shock as icy water splashes my face. Sawyer yells at us to paddle hard but keeping my oar in the water as I'm tossed around is nearly impossible.

Finally, the water mellows out, becoming smooth and tranquil once again.

"Wow!" Josie squeals. "That was awesome!" She clings to Ryan's arm. "And I didn't even fall in!"

"Way to go!" He grins.

"How tough were those rapids?" I ask Sawyer.

"Category Three. Now, if you really want a thrill ride you should head to Gore Canyon, at the steepest section of the

Colorado River. It drops about three hundred feet within three miles—so intense. During the snow melt in the spring, the rapids are usually Class Five or even higher."

Wow—I can't imagine how difficult more intense rapids would be. I cringe at the thought but notice the gleam in Jake's eye. Maybe he can ask Ryan to join in that adventure—sounds a little too extreme for me.

Back at the ranch, Sam and Annabelle beg us to swim with them. Ryan and I tell them no, knowing how annoying our siblings can be. But Jake and Josie are not immune to their pathetic puppy dog eyes and agree. Maybe I should have a little sympathy—who would want to spend their whole vacation with just the grown-ups?

Josie and I watch from the luxury of the lounge chairs while the others jump in the pool. Soon they have created some type of volleyball game. Annabelle sits on Jake's shoulders while Sam is perched on Ryan's. They are attempting to bat a beach ball back and forth without letting it hit the water. When the game ends, Jake and Ryan begin a back-flip competition off the diving board. No need to watch...I really doubt Ryan has a chance to win this one. Jake spends his life doing mid-air flips and spins. Time to make my exit and get cleaned up for dinner.

As I'm shampooing my hair, I think of those men. No logical explanation comes to mind as to why they would be changing their appearance. They must be up to no good.

After we've all showered and changed, the others agree that it's finally time to tell someone about our suspicions. We track down Lee and Lola in the lodge at one of the tables. Paperwork is spread out in front of them.

Since it was my idea, I take the lead. "Excuse me, can we

talk to you both for a moment?"

Lola pushes away her pile. "Of course. Did you have fun rafting?"

"Absolutely, it was fantastic."

"You kids might like going down to Glenwood while you're here. The hot springs are always popular."

Before the conversation veers off to other sightseeing spots, I decide to take back control of the conversation. "Did you know that Glenwood Springs was originally named Defiance, Colorado?"

Lee gives me an appreciative nod. "That's right. A great name for an Old West town."

My mouth continues blurting out information. "The wife of the man who founded the town really missed Iowa, so she renamed Defiance after her hometown, Glenwood." I bite my lip. I really should've had a plan instead of just winging this.

Jake winks at me. "We actually do want to talk to you about something."

I send him a thankful smile then explain our concerns about the men we'd seen.

Lee rubs his whiskery chin. "That is indeed strange."

Lola covers his hand with hers. "We should call the sheriff and let him check it out."

"Where did you say their camp was located?" Lee asks.

"From the top of the four-wheel trail you suggested, we could see the camp down below in the valley," Jake explains.

Lee nods. "I know where you mean. I'll give the Sheriff a call right now." He stands and makes his way into his office.

Lola smiles at us. "Do you think we should tell your parents?"

"No."

Her eyebrows raise at our unanimous chorus.

I laugh. "We'll let them know after the sheriff finds out what's going on." Parents have a habit of overreacting. Especially my dad who tries to plan for every possible scenario. He'd probably make us keep a chaperone with us for the rest of the trip.

Lola smiles. "All right then. Well, you've got some time before dinner. Any plans?"

"Horseback riding," Ryan states.

I glance at Jake and see the gleam in his eye and know what he's thinking. "No." I tell them both. "We can go on a ride but you two are not racing."

Lola nods. "Sorry, boys, these horses like to follow the trails at a leisurely pace."

"Fine," they answer in unison.

They look like adolescent boys with their identical, defeated expressions.

We leave the lodge, glad to have someone else worry about the men, and make our way to the stables. One of the ranch hands helps us choose horses for our ride. Despite the man's reluctance, Josie insists on riding the one named Prima Donna for our intended leisurely ride.

a GENT MARTINEZ LOWERED his pen. "Then what happened?"

Sophie crinkled her forehead. "That's when Ryan tried to have me thrown from my horse."

"Excuse me?"

"We were enjoying a nice peaceful ride, just the four of us, wandering along the trail, through the forest, admiring the views. Well, it was supposed to be peaceful and it would've been if Ryan and Jake had behaved."

Agent Martinez reached for his mug. "I thought they agreed not to race the horses."

The moment the words popped out of his mouth he regretted them. Why did he care? How were these kids sucking him into their lives? He lifted the mug to take a swig of coffee and focus back on this case. He grimaced. The mug was empty.

Sophie didn't seem to notice his inner turmoil and continued to talk. "Well, they technically didn't race but they each kept trying to edge their horse into the lead, destroying my peaceful ride. I finally had enough and nudged my horse forward to move ahead of them both. Then instead of competing with Jake, Ryan rode his horse close to mine. I'm not sure if he was trying to take the lead again or simply wanted to annoy me but whatever the reason, my horse lost patience as well and galloped forward, nearly knocking me off. I had to cling to the saddle horn."

Agent Martinez rubbed his brow to ward off the

headache that crept across his temple.

Sophie watched him. "Don't worry, I was okay. But that's when we noticed that Josie was nowhere in sight. As our three horses kept moving faster and faster, hers decided to keep the slow pace we'd started with. She tried to get it to pick up speed, but it just meandered at its own pokey pace. The horse should've been named Molasses. We spent a good chunk of the afternoon waiting on Josie and Prima Donna."

She finally bit her lip and stopped talking.

"I see. Getting back to the case. Why didn't you want to tell your parents about the men?"

"Oh. Well, we didn't really know if anything was actually going on or if it was just our imaginations. So we figured it was best if the sheriff checked into it first."

Agent Martinez reached for his notebook.

"Besides, I don't think my parents would've been very excited to find out we were investigating something again. They haven't been too thrilled with the cases Jake and I have accidentally found ourselves entangled in."

Agent Martinez nodded. "Yes, I remember reading in the paper about some of your adventures."

Sophie sighed. "We don't try to get mixed up in these things. Trouble just sort of follows us."

He rubbed his jaw. Why couldn't these kids simply get to the information he needed? "Sounds like the four of you have a lot of fun together."

She smiled. "We do. Good friends just make life more enjoyable."

He shut his notebook and gave her a curt nod. Then he pushed away from the table and stood.

"Agent Martinez?"

He looked at her.

"I hope I'm not totally out of place here, but family and friends are really important. I can't help but worry about you spending every weekend at your cabin alone."

He rubbed his eyebrow, trying to stop the twitch of annoyance.

"Sorry, I don't mean to offend you. I just had this strong feeling I should say something and pray for you."

Was she serious? Who says that to an FBI agent?

She shrugged. "Does God ever talk to you like that? Give you a strong feeling that you can't shake?"

"I need more coffee." He exited the interrogation room and made his way to the lounge again.

He poured the remaining caffeinated sludge into this mug. These kids were getting to him. Did she really feel a need to pray for him or was she messing with him? She had no need to play mind games—it wasn't like she was in trouble.

He took a swig of coffee as he thought about what Sophie had said regarding friendships and how important they were. He used to have good friends but moving every couple of years and trying to repair a crumbling marriage made maintaining those connections difficult. Hearing these kids talk somehow made him nostalgic for the old days and forgotten relationships. He shook his head—must be getting soft in his old age.

He begrudgingly glanced at the clock. So much for Friday night at the lake. He'd have to settle for Saturday and Sunday. He probably could've tried to hurry these kids' statements along, but he'd discovered over the years it was better to let the witnesses tell their tales at their own pace. When they elaborated on their stories of their own accord, they often added more facts and elements than they would have otherwise. But he'd never experienced a group of teens quite like these four.

Agent Martinez took his replenished mug and trudged down the hall to the last interrogation room. When he opened the door, the teenage boy sitting at the table stood and held out his hand.

"Hi, I'm Jake."

Agent Martinez shook the hand of the reigning halfpipe silver medalist. "Yes, I know who you are. It seems like trouble has a way of following you."

"Don't believe everything you read." The kid's gaze shifted to the table then back up to meet his.

"You've had a few unusual experiences." With a nod of his head, Martinez motioned for Jake to sit back down then took the seat across from him.

Jake's eyebrows raised slightly. "I guess that's what happens when you attempt to do the right thing. I try to use my fame to be a good role model, so when I see injustices I just can't let them go."

Huh. The agent hadn't expected that.

Jake seemed unnerved by the silence and kept talking. "Don't get me wrong. I didn't always think like that. Instant fame was difficult, but Sophie got me back on track and encouraged me to join her youth group. That's when things changed."

Church again? What was it with these kids? Did good kids still exist out there? All he ever saw in these rooms were the troublemakers.

Jake shifted in his seat. "I figured out that when you get away from church and people with similar morals, you lose your focus on what's important and suddenly other things become the center of your life."

Like fishing?

Agent Martinez cleared his throat. "Well, it's nice to meet you Jake. I'm sorry to have kept you waiting. I chatted first with Josie, Ryan and Sophie. Now I'd like to get your statement."

Jake kept his hands on his lap, a technique the agent himself used to control his fidgeting. Jake probably picked it up over the years while dealing with reporters. "Of course, sir. What would you like to know?"

He preformed his brief recap once again, making sure all the stories matched.

"Okay, I think I'm pretty well caught up on the events leading up to today. Maybe you could tell me everything that happened from this morning until you arrived here." Agent Martinez flipped to a new page in his notebook.

"Sure." The famous teen looked down and studied the table. "Let's see, I guess it started with Josie setting Ryan's dad's hat on fire."

The agent looked up at the young snowboarding superstar. Why was getting to the bottom of this case so difficult?

Jake grinned. "Well, she didn't mean to. Josie's ... unique. Always jumping in with both feet before testing the waters."

The agent reached for his mug. He might have to brew a whole new pot to get through this night. "Is this relevant somehow?"

"Kinda. Because of that we decided to get away and go hiking."

Part 4
Jake

*J*OSIE BRUSHES PAST me and plops down next to Lee. "You're sure the Sheriff didn't find them?"

We're gathered around the outside firepit where breakfast is being served this morning. The aroma of the sizzling bacon makes my mouth water. Could anything be better than an old-school chuckwagon cookout to start the day? I doubt it. Since the morning's a little cool, everyone is circled around the roaring fire.

Lee stretches out his long legs and crosses his scuffed cowboy boots at the ankle. "Nope, sorry. He did search the area where you said you'd seen those men, and he could tell someone had been camping at that spot, but they're gone now."

Our four sets of eyes dart between each other. Worry lines cross Sophie's face.

"Well, thanks for having him check it out," I tell him.

"Sure. Better to be safe." He pats Josie's knee. "By the way, sweetheart, thanks for the beautiful music last night. Your duet with Vince soothed my soul."

She beams at his praise. "Thank you. It was really fun. I wish we were staying longer and I had time to teach him a few of my favorite tunes. Him singing 'Oh What a Beautiful Morning' from *Oklahoma* would be standing-ovation worthy."

"Guess you'll have to come again. Now if you'll excuse me." He stands and strides over to talk to Sophie's grandpa.

Ryan leans forward, forearms resting on his knees.

"Looks like our mystery has come to an end."

Sophie crinkles her forehead.

I know that look. It's one I've become all too familiar with. She suspects something sinister and is not going to let it drop.

I squeeze her hand. "Bloomers, we tried. But if they left town, there's nothing more we can do. Case closed."

"I suppose, but I know they were up to no good."

Josie nods, her ponytail bobbing in agreement. "They were totally acting as fishy as the conmen in *Kiss Me Kate*."

I shoot a look at Sophie. She turns her head, trying to hide her grin. Josie and her musical references. Sophie and I joke that maybe we should start some kind of game to go along with the theater references. I'm thinking maybe a pushup for each time she brings up a musical. Seems like an easy way to get in an extra workout.

Josie stands with an exaggerated sigh. "I'm so bummed. I really thought we were onto something."

She spins around to carry her tin plate and silverware to the dirty dish cart but trips over the camp dog lying next to her chair. Chaos suddenly spreads like a rash. As she flies through the air in a surprisingly graceful way, everything she's holding leaves her hands, soaring right along with her. Her plate becomes a flying disc that smacks into the side of Sam's leg. The kid springs out of his seat, dumping cocoa onto his mom's lap. She's so startled she flings eggs into Annabelle's hair. Annabelle lets out a bloodcurdling scream, startling Grandpa Frank who spills coffee down the front of his shirt. Ryan's dad knocks his chair over when he leaps up to help. At the sudden movement, his cowboy hat, which had been resting on his knee, sails into the fire.

We all watch the prized possession sizzle and burn to a

crisp.

For a moment no one says a word. Absolute silence.

"Oh no!" Josie, still sprawled across the ground, finally gasps.

Ryan helps her up and suddenly everyone bursts out in laughter. Everyone except Josie.

"Oh, my gosh, I'm so sorry. I'll buy you a new one."

Ryan's dad walks through the path of destruction toward her. "Are you all right?"

"Yes, but I feel so bad about your hat. You were so proud of it."

He shakes his head, and the lopsided grin that he and Ryan share spreads across his face. "I'll never figure out how someone so prone to accidents can be such a glorious dancer on stage."

Josie's face turns as red as the bandana tied around the dog's neck. She shrugs. "One of the wonders of me, I guess."

I glance at Sophie again. Maybe for each of Josie's clumsy incidents we could do a sit up. The Josie workout could be quite effective.

Josie brushes the dirt off the front of her clothes. "Let me help you all clean up."

"No!" A chorus of voices ring out in unison.

Lola drapes her arm around Josie's shoulder. "Don't worry dear, we've got this."

"Okay, if you're sure." She turns back to Sophie and me with a sheepish look. "Well, that added some excitement to the morning."

Ryan comes up behind her and wraps his arms around her. "Your mom would've loved that one."

She rolls her eyes. "Yep, that would've made it into her next book for sure. Well, what should we do today? Hang out around here?"

Sophie shakes her head. "Maybe it would be best if we got away for a while. We could go on a hike."

I'd be down for that. "Sounds great." Although I wonder about our chances of making it through a hike without Josie hurting herself. She certainly brings some entertainment to everything we do.

Lee tells us about a great hiking path to a picturesque waterfall. Sophie's eyes sparkle at the word "picturesque." After promising Annabelle and Sam another afternoon at the pool, the four of us climb into my Jeep and drive the short distance to the trailhead.

Our hike starts out at a nice leisurely pace up a tree-lined path, but then I notice Ryan pulling slightly ahead. I quicken my steps. The girls linger behind, chatting. Or, more accurately, Josie peppering Sophie with questions about the plays and musicals our school theater department put on this past year. Josie had discovered that Sophie takes photos of all the school activities for the yearbook and attends some rehearsals and performances. Now she wants to hear all about the program.

At a narrow section of the path, Ryan moves in front of me. I lengthen my stride and when the path veers to the left, I make a move on the inside of the turn to take the lead.

"Boys," Sophie calls. "Can't you give the competition a rest for one day?"

"Nope." Ryan and I answer in unison.

Ryan speed walks, trying to move back into the lead. Nope. Don't think so. Soon we're jogging. I shoot him a grin and then take off.

I don't know what it is about the two of us, but we can't seem to control our cut-throat one-upmanship. I don't have a lot of friends my age. My teammates are all older, and my friend Chad would rather play his guitar or skateboard than compete with me. So it's fun to have Ryan around.

"Don't think so, Taylor," he says, keeping my pace.

Soon we're sprinting up the path, leaping over fallen logs, dodging boulders. I'm not worried though. I have the advantage. Because the path is heading up a mountain and since I live here, the altitude won't bother me as much as it will him.

I hear him gasping for breath and know I'm about to be the victor. That's when we burst through a clearing and come upon a campsite with two tents.

We skid to a stop.

The campers look up from the campfire they're sitting around and stare at us.

The first thing I notice is the unusually black hair on one of the guys. The one next to him has a buzz cut. My gaze goes to his massive arms and the snake tattoo on his bicep. The men we've been seeing around. Sophie was right, they've tried to change their appearance. They've obviously decided on a new campsite. No wonder the sheriff couldn't find them.

Ryan raises his hand like he's going to apologize, but no words come out as he's still trying to catch his breath.

"Hey," I say to the four men watching us. "Sorry, man. We were just hiking, didn't know there was a campsite here. Sorry to barge in."

Our archery-site friend narrows his eyes. We turn to leave right as the girls arrive.

"There you are," Josie says. "You two missed all the beautiful—"

Ryan grabs her arm and spins her away from the

campsite.

Before I can reroute Sophie, recognition flickers in her eyes as she spots the men.

"Again, sorry to disturb you. We'll find another path," I call over my shoulder. Then I grab Sophie's arm and pull her back into the woods.

We start down the trail in single file with Sophie in the lead. When she abruptly stops, I have to dodge around her to keep from plowing her over. That's when I notice the spark of curiosity in her eyes. Suddenly, I have a really bad feeling about whatever is swirling around in that pretty head of hers.

I reach for her hand. "Soph, come on. Let's keep going."

She shakes her hand loose. "Those are the guys." Her tone further triggers my unease.

"Obviously." I pull out my cell phone. Time to involve the professionals. Unfortunately, there's no reception. New plan. "Let's drive into town and tell the sheriff where to find them."

"But what if we spooked them and they move their camp again? I have my camera." She holds it up, as if I need proof. "I should sneak back and get a photo. That way the sheriff will know what they look like and can keep an eye on them if they come into town."

Josie nods. "That makes sense."

I shake my head, not liking the idea. "That guy from the archery incident already looked suspicious. I don't think we should risk going back."

Sophie's not buying my argument. "If he's suspicious of us *and* up to no good, then he'll definitely leave town. This might be our only chance to help the sheriff."

I glance at Ryan, hoping he'll be on my side, but he shrugs. "You both make good points."

Sophie holds up her camera again. "And I don't have to get too close, I can use my lens to zoom in."

I sigh, knowing I've lost the argument. When she gets an idea in her head there's no talking her out of it.

Sophie smiles her victory. We veer off the path and slowly inch our way through the thick woods, circling back toward the camp.

As I steal through the trees and shrubs, I feel the cold metal of my confirmation cross against my chest. It reassures me, and I can't help a smile, despite my unease.

Please God, help us. Keep us safe.

The men's voices reach us before we see them.

"I'm telling you, those are the kids that nearly shot me with an arrow."

"So what? We're bound to run into people up here. It's not like they know anything."

We move slowly, careful to stay out of view.

"Maybe we should move camp, just to be on the safe side."

"From what? Some meddling kids? This isn't Scooby Doo."

That got a few chuckles from the other men.

"Besides," another voice chimes in. "We have to wait on Brooks for the stuff. He should be here any minute."

Sophie and I exchange looks. I know exactly what she's thinking—that we should stay and get photos of this Brooks and the mysterious "stuff." I turn to look at Ryan and Josie. They both nod. I'm not crazy about the idea but majority rules.

Sophie inches forward then crouches down and rests the camera on her knee. She adjusts the lens and takes a few shots. As the rest of us gingerly move forward to get a visual,

81

we hear the sound of a truck driving on gravel. There must be a road nearby.

One of the men stands. "That must be Brooks now."

"Good. This whole process has taken longer than I thought it would. Staying around in one spot is making me nervous."

A car door slams.

Soon another man emerges from the woods and into their campsite.

Josie's breath catches, and she clutches Ryan's arm. "That's the guy who works at the pawn shop."

We watch the pawn shop owner open a duffel bag and pass out small bundles to each of the men. I'm too far away to make out the contents.

"Okay," he says. "Here's all that you need."

"Nice doing business with you."

Maybe whatever they wanted to pawn off sold, and he brought them their money.

"Listen," Brooks says. "I don't know why, but Sheriff Jones paid me a visit and was asking questions about some unusual men in town. Something must have tipped him off. If I were you, I'd separate. Each of you should make your own way out of the area—and soon."

Sophie looks at me, her eyes wide. Her instincts were right. Something illegal must be going on. Why else would they care about the sheriff?

Our archery friend jumps up. "I bet it's those kids. I told you something was wrong with them."

"What kids?" Brooks asks.

"I had a run-in with some teenagers the other day. And we just saw them a few minutes ago, when they burst in on us, right here at this camp."

Mr. Bad Dye Job jumps in. "They nearly shot him with arrows when he stole that calf."

One of the other men leans back in his chair. "Still seems like a stupid thing to steal. Who knew a stupid cow was worth so much."

"Yeah, I would've preferred eatin' the dumb thing than selling it."

The archery guy leans forward. "Hey, we needed the money. I don't remember any of you coming up with a better way to get it."

The shop owner glances around. "Wait. Back up. Were the teenagers two couples?"

"Yep."

He scratches his head. "They came into my shop right after you did the other day."

"That can't be no coincidence."

"They're probably still around here somewhere. Let's search for them." The fourth guy chimes in.

"And what are you going to do if you find them?" asks Brooks.

"Nothing I haven't done before."

A chill zips down my spine.

"Don't be stupid. You need to get out of the area." Brooks points to one of the pouches he'd just delivered. "You have all you need to disappear. Be smart and leave. Now I have a few more supplies for you in my truck. Two of you—come with me to get them."

I grab Sophie's arm and nod in the opposite direction. We need to get out of here before they change their minds.

She shakes her head. "Aren't you curious as to what's in those pouches he gave them?"

I see the wheels in her head turning. "Soph, no. We need

to leave."

She ignores me and turns to Ryan and Josie. "What do you guys think?"

Ryan glances at me. "I'm with Jake. Those guys have a vicious edge to them. We need to go talk to the sheriff."

Josie shakes her head. "But these guys are ready to leave town. By the time we talk to Sheriff Jones and convince him to come investigate, they'll be long gone."

"Good. Then they'll be someone else's problem." I don't give a rip about what they're up to. I just want to keep our hides safe.

Sophie tilts her head and raises her eyebrows at me. "Jake. Seriously? It'll be someone else's problem? You, who risked everything to stop a major drug operation, want to just let these men go?"

"This is different. We don't even know if they've done anything wrong besides steal that calf. The theft of one cow is bad, but it's not a danger to the community."

"They must be up to no good if they needed to change their appearances and needed burner phones," Josie argues.

"But we have no proof of anything."

"Then let's get it," Josie urges. "I could pretend to be lost and wander back into their camp to catch a glimpse of those bundles."

"No." Ryan answers. "That's insane. We don't know what these guys are capable of."

Finally, a voice of reason.

"There are only two of them right now. You and Jake could overpower them if you needed to." She's not giving up.

"Not if they have weapons." I haven't given in yet either.

Sophie turns back to watch the camp through her lens. "I

guess you're right. I just hate for them to disappear if they are criminals."

"We'll show the sheriff your photos, so he knows what to look for. Plus, we can tell him that the pawn shop owner is involved somehow."

Josie pulls out her phone. "And I'll keep checking my cell. Sooner or later we'll get a signal and can call someone."

Sophie sighs. "Okay."

We start making our way through the woods towards the path, trying not to make a sound.

A GENT MARTINEZ GLANCED from his empty mug to Jake.

"Did you finally get through to Sheriff Jones?"

Jake leaned back in his chair. "Yes, when we got closer to where the Jeep was parked. But the receptionist didn't seem interested, so I also called the dude ranch and spoke to Lola. She said she knew the sheriff and would contact him directly."

Agent Martinez stared down at his hands. He didn't like the witnesses to interact and possibly contaminate the story, but it was getting late. Talking to each of them individually was taking forever, so he made a decision.

"Wait right here. I'm going to gather the others then we can finish this interview."

Entering the break room, he picked up the coffee pot, wishing for something a lot stronger than black coffee. He tipped the pot over his mug but not a drop came out. Great.

On his way back to Jake's interrogation room, Agent Martinez stopped at the closed doors along the way and gathered all the teenagers. Josie clung to Ryan as they followed him down the hall. Sophie walked right beside him.

"Do you have enough information? Are we free to go?" she asked.

He shook his head and kept walking. "Not quite yet."

"Where's Jake?"

He didn't answer, just stopped at a door and swung it open. When Sophie stepped inside, Jake stood, and she hurried into his embrace. Agent Martinez shook his head. Young love—untainted and full of promise. If only it could stay that way. He and Maggie once looked at each other like that.

He stood at the head of table. "Please take a seat. Your statements all seem to be consistent, so in the interest of time, I'd like to hear the rest of the story with you all together."

The four teenagers sat in the metal chairs. Josie inched her chair as close to Ryan's as physically possible.

"Jake told me how you witnessed the pawn shop owner delivering packages to the men at their camp. Then you called the sheriff and Lola. Is that correct?"

They all nod. So far so good.

"Great. Then what happened?"

Ryan was the first to respond. "We started down the path toward Jake's Jeep."

Josie shook her head back and forth. "First, we actually argued about whether or not we should sneak into the camp to try and find out what was in the packages."

"No," Sophie said. "That discussion happened before Jake made the phone call."

"But I remember there was something we couldn't agree on while we tried to find the path," Josie persisted.

Jake jumped in. "That's right. We debated whether it was safe to take the path down or if we should stay hidden in the trees."

"Right." Sophie looked at Agent Martinez. "Josie and I thought the path would be better, so we could get down faster. The boys insisted on staying in the woods."

Josie's head bobbed in agreement. "Oh, that's right. How could I forget?" She crossed her arms. "They, of course, got their way even though Sophie and I were right."

Ryan threw her a look. "It would've worked out just fine if Sophie hadn't insisted on stopping and taking a photo of that pond."

"Wait a minute." Sophie leaned forward. "Snapping that photo would've taken a few seconds at the most. You and Josie were the ones who wanted to stop and take selfies by the water."

Josie tilted her head toward Agent Martinez. "And here I thought he was being all romantic when really he'd just found another way to annoy Sophie."

Sophie twitched from a shiver. "Don't think I forgot, Ryan. My revenge will be coming."

"Stop!" Agent Martinez rubbed his temples. This might have been a bad idea. He needed to redirect them. But despite his better judgement, he was somewhat curious what Ryan's latest prank had been.

No. It doesn't matter. Stand firm. Stick to the facts.

"I don't really care about your walk in the woods. When did you run into the men again?"

Josie stared at him like he was clueless. "Well, we were coming to that part of the story."

Jake leaned forward. "The point is that we took a little longer to get down to the Jeep than if we had simply taken the path."

"Like *we* had suggested," Josie added.

Sophie gave her a darn-right-sister look then turned back to Agent Martinez. "As we neared the Jeep, we heard voices, so we found a spot where we could get a better look at whoever was talking."

Josie squirmed in her seat. "We were standing by this little cliff..."

Ryan turned to her and shook his head. "Not really a cliff, just a small ridge."

Jake nodded. "I'd say more of a steep rockface."

"Yeah," Ryan agreed. "There wasn't a huge drop off."

Josie rolled her eyes. "If you two are done with your mansplaining, I can get on with the story. Anyway, there was this…bluff thing we were on. We could peek through the trees and see down to the Jeep. A truck was parked nearby. The pawn shop owner and two of the guys were standing around talking."

Ryan leaned back in his chair. "And that's when things went downhill."

"Literally." Jake shot a smirk towards Ryan.

Josie glared at both of them. "Don't blame this on me. This was Ryan's fault."

Sophie nodded. "I'm gonna have to agree with Josie on this one."

Agent Martinez dropped his head in his hands. He didn't realize he had actually groaned until silence filled the room. He peeked out at the group of teens, who were all watching him. He straightened up, reminding himself that he'd soon be done with them—if only they could get through this story.

He cleared his throat. "Can we just stick to the facts? Jake, can you—and you alone—tell me what happened next?"

Jake

WHEN WE REACH the end of the woods, we are greeted by the murmur of voices. Dread creeps through my veins. We edge close to the ridge overlooking the clearing where we'd parked the Jeep. My suspicion is confirmed. Making sure to stay hidden amid the bushes, we watch the men examine the Jeep. Their low voices make it hard to hear what they're saying, but whatever it is probably isn't good. If we hadn't taken the detour to the pond, we'd be on our way to the sheriff's office right now. But we hadn't felt the urgency. Until now. With these guys standing guard, we can't get to the Jeep and get out of here. There's nothing to do but wait them out.

Sophie peers through her camera then lets it hang around her neck by the strap. She scrunches her face in frustration before reaching for her camera case—probably to get her telephoto lens.

Suddenly, everything happens in a blur of movement. As she digs in the case, Ryan lurches toward her, causing Josie to take a step backwards, closer to the edge of the ledge. Sophie's eyes pop open and her hand jerks out of the camera bag, flinging something in the air.

I watch in stunned silence. A small green object that looks like a frog sails past me to land on Josie's hair. She starts batting at it with both hands, too wrapped up in having a spastic fit to notice when the frog leaps off and hops away.

Surprisingly, she's able to keep herself from screaming—but in her manic attempt to get away from the frog, she takes another step backwards. The edge of the ridge gives way, crumbling beneath her feet. Before any of us can react, she tumbles down the hill. We watch in horror as she rolls, a cloud of dust following her down the steep embankment. She comes to an abrupt landing at the feet of the three men.

For a moment nothing happens. Josie lies there stunned. The men stand staring at her. We silently observe from above.

An angry Sophie smacks Ryan. "This really wasn't the time for a prank," she hisses.

Ryan squeezes his eyes shut. "I couldn't help myself when I saw those big eyes staring up at me at the pond. How would I know you'd decide to root through your camera bag again?"

"Don't blame me. This is not my fault."

I elbow them both to keep them quiet. The man they called Brooks glances in our direction, but we stay crouched behind the bushes.

Josie turns her head and looks up at the three men standing over her. "Sorry for dropping in. I guess I just lost my footing. I tend to be a bit of a klutz."

They don't appear too happy to see her.

"This is one of those kids."

"Let's take her back to camp. We'll decide what to do with her there."

One of the men grabs her arm and yanks her up.

"Hey! That hurts!" She yells. "Get your meaty paws off of me!"

I clamp onto Ryan's arm but there's no stopping him. He tears down the hill after her.

"Let go of her!"

I can only imagine how he must feel, seeing them manhandle his girl, but what's he thinking? He's outnumbered. Should I run down and help?

One of the other men whips out a gun from behind his back and points it at Ryan.

Nope. Definitely not the time to run into the fray.

Ryan raises his hands. "Whoa. I'm just coming to check on my girlfriend."

Sophie looks at me, her eyes big pools of abject terror.

Think. *Hey, a little help here God?*

No sooner do I ask when an idea pops into my head. *Thanks, God.* I nod to the side, and we edge through the trees while Ryan tries to convince the men that he and Josie were innocently hiking when she lost her footing. With them as a distraction, I concentrate on my plan. If we circle around behind the men, we might have the element of surprise. We inch close enough to hear the discussion.

"Stop talking!" one of the guys demands.

"Let's just take them back to camp. We can interrogate them there," his friend chimes in.

"Yeah, I guess that makes the most sense," Brooks agrees.

Not if I can help it. We need to stop them now while there are only three of them.

The men are still facing the Jeep. The truck is behind them—and so are Sophie and I. As we silently slink toward their vehicle, Ryan catches my eye. He reaches out his hands into a plea.

"Wait. I don't know what you think the problem is, but we just came here to hike. We don't want any trouble. Just let us go, and we'll be out of your hair and on our way."

"Yeah." Josie throws a little bravado into her tone.

"Why'd you go all villainy on us anyway? I just fell down, which happens all the time. I didn't even land on you, but I still said I was sorry."

While Ryan and Josie attempt to plead their case, the guys are momentarily occupied. I crouch and keep watch from behind the truck while Sophie opens her camera case and moves to the side furthest from the men. We always joke about how her overprotective dad insists she carry certain items in her bag—to be prepared for any emergency. I'll have to thank him for his foresight.

A soft hiss of air tells me she's used her pocketknife and stabbed the tires. I stealthily climb into the bed of the truck. Before Sophie can cause any more damage, the men—who weren't buying Ryan and Josie's excuses—force them toward the vehicle.

Peering through the sliding rear window, I'm relieved to see the guy with the gun no longer has his weapon pointed at Ryan. He must have stuck it into the back of his jeans again. Now he has an iron grip on Ryan's arm. The other two men walk next to each other, one of them holding Josie's elbow.

As they approach, I spring up onto the roof, then leap off the cab of the truck, spinning in the air—like I do on the halfpipe—to increase my momentum.

Completely confused, they freeze.

I spiral toward them and manage a savage split kick into their chests. It's not enough to knock them down, but they stagger backward, stunned. Sophie rushes into the fray with an aerosol can and spews pepper spray in their faces.

Our one-two punch leaves them incapacitated.

The men bend over, temporarily blinded by the chemicals. Miserable groans testify to their agony. Not sure how, but Ryan gets away from the guy holding him. He must have fought him off during my surprise attack. Since he's closest to our getaway vehicle, I toss him my keys and turn to help Josie, but she's already scurrying toward the Jeep. Her captor must have released his grip when Sophie sprayed him. I bring up the rear as the girls scramble into the Jeep and leap inside as Ryan floors the accelerator and speeds away.

*A*GENT MARTINEZ CONTEMPLATED Jake's story, especially the part where he'd prayed for guidance. How long had it been since he'd done that himself?

"Wait." Josie shook her head. "That's not quite how I remember it going down. After my unfortunate tumble down the hill, those men yanked my arm really hard and pulled me up. They started badgering me with questions. I was coming up with an escape plan when Ryan stormed down the hill to rescue me." She leaned her head on his shoulder. "My knight in shining armor."

Ryan kisses the top of her head.

"Anyway, as we were trying to talk our way out of the situation, we saw Jake and Sophie sneak into the clearing near the truck. The men wouldn't believe our story. They dragged us toward the vehicle. I don't know what their plan was, but I sure didn't want to find out. We neared the truck and Jake and Sophie jumped out. I think they really shook those guys up!"

She grinned, and Martinez found his lips curving upward—just a little—despite himself.

"That's when Ryan swung around and punched the guy who was holding his arm. One smack right in the jaw was all it took. Ryan was the closest to our vehicle, so Jake threw the car keys to him. He snagged the keys out of the air and bolted toward the Jeep. The man he'd punched swung toward him. I was so afraid he'd use the gun! I grabbed a branch and whacked him on the head. As Ryan neared the passenger side of the Jeep, he slid like he does into home plate—right under the high wheel-based Jeep. He popped up on the driver's side, jumped in and started the engine. The rest of us piled in and he tore out of there."

Sophie stared at her. "Well, that's partially right...I guess. But you're missing the part about why Jake threw the keys to Ryan. Jake was dealing with two of the men by himself so had to toss the keys to Ryan." She sent her boyfriend a dewy-eyed look. "It was like one of those action movies when the hero's in a two-on-one battle. Jake was...just...amazing! I tried to help a little by dousing the guys with my pepper spray after they were already down."

Ryan stopped his cousin. "Hold on. I'll admit you two did a fantastic job, but don't forget how Josie handled the guy with the gun. When I reached the Jeep, I turned around and saw her doing dance moves or something on the poor unsuspecting bad guy."

Josie beamed. "It was actually the choreographed fight scene from *West Side Story*. I hit him on the head with the branch then aimed for his ankles and finished with a jump kick into his side. I can't wait to tell my drama teacher how well it worked. And of course, Sophie blasted him with the pepper spray."

Agent Martinez looked back and forth between them all. Somewhere in the mix of their stories lie the actual truth. Good enough. He was almost afraid to ask the next question. "And then what happened?"

Sophie answered first. "Part way down the road, we met up with the sheriff. He had spoken to Lola and was driving up to check on the situation. We told him what had happened, and he asked us to meet him back at his station while he and his deputy went on to capture the bad guys."

Josie nodded. "We were at the station, waiting for the sheriff, when one of the agents from your office brought us here."

Jake turned toward Agent Martinez. "That's all we know. Can you fill us in on who those men were?"

"And why we were questioned all afternoon by the FBI?" Ryan added.

Agent Martinez nodded. He'd gladly fill them in. Gladly! He'd never been so happy to be done with an interview. "Well, it turns out you uncovered an operation to smuggle criminals out of the country. The four men you were suspicious of are all wanted men, on the run. Trey Brooks, the pawnbroker, is part of a network that leads criminals to freedom—for a price. If the criminals have enough to pay him or trade him, he provides weapons, clothing, disguises, and fake IDs. This has been going on for a while, but we hadn't been able to track them down. So, on behalf of the Federal Bureau of Investigation, thank you for your assistance."

"Do we get some kind of special medal or something?" Josie asked.

"No. However, I do believe some reporters are waiting outside for a statement."

Jake groaned. "Seriously?"

Sophie squeezed his hand. "Is there a back way out?"

"Oh, come on guys." Josie smoothed her hair down. "It might be fun."

Agent Martinez stood, ready to leave the four of them to their discussion. If he worked late to file his report, he might still get in nearly two full days of fishing at the cabin.

Except it didn't sound quite as fun anymore. He glanced

at his witnesses, envious of their friendship. Maybe they were right, and he should reach out to some folks. This weekend he'd fish on Saturday then...maybe make it to church on Sunday.

Some of his old friends might even remember him.

Yeah, he'd give it a try.

Thank you for reading *Unlikely Witnesses*. This story is a reminder that if we live our lives as Christians, we never know when we might be a witness for Christ. If you enjoyed this novella, I would be grateful if you'd recommend it to others and/or write a quick review.

I've had a lot of fun with these four characters. In fact, they appear together in a few other short stories, as well as their individual full-length novels. If you're interested in more adventures with Jake, Sophie, Ryan and Josie, please check out my award-winning novels. Here is the chronological order of all their stories.

Shared Blessings – the winter of their sophomore year of high school.

This free short story is a gift to those who sign-up for my newsletter at www.LesleaWahl.com. The four characters are first introduced in this interconnected tale through a unique artifact.

An Unexpected Role – the summer between their sophomore and junior years

Josie and Ryan appear in this recipient of a Moonbeam Children's Book Award.

After a humiliating event and overwhelming peer pressure, 16-year-old Josie flees her home to spend the summer with her aunt on a South Carolina island. Her fresh start turns into the summer of her dreams as friendships grow, romance blossoms, and a series of thefts surround her with excitement. However, when tragedy strikes someone close to her, Josie comes to understand there are more important things than her reputation. As she sets out to solve the mystery she has become entangled in, she not only realizes the importance of relying on her faith but along the way also discovers who God wants her to be.

Perfect Blindside – the fall of their junior year of high school

This is the first novel that I wrote and is the story of Jake and Sophie. *Perfect Blindside* has won numerous awards including a Catholic Press Association Award, a Readers' Favorite Award, and an Illumination Children's Book Award.

Fresh off a championship medal, Jake Taylor's parents have dragged him to a middle-of-nowhere town in Colorado, far from where he wants to be. Smart and savvy, Sophie has spent the summer before her junior year of high school avidly following Jake Taylor in every article she can find, but now she sees the "truth" behind the story — he's really a jerk. When the only thing they can see is each other's flaws, how can Jake and Sophie work together to figure out what's been happening at the abandoned silver mine? Follow Sophie and Jake into secret tunnels as they unravel the mystery and challenge each other to become who God wants them to be.

eXtreme Blindside – the winter of their junior year of high school

eXtreme Blindside is the exciting continuation to *Perfect Blindside* and delves into the topic of putting God first in your life.

After winning silver, teen snowboarder Jake Taylor struggles with sudden fame. Then he's offered a gig he can't refuse: becoming a spokesperson for a state-of-the-art athletic training facility. Preparing for its first competition, Jake's faith—and his fame—allow him to help others when, one by one, athletes are mysteriously sabotaged. Time is running out for Jake and his girlfriend, Sophie, to figure out what is going on before he is also sabotaged...or worse.

More Precious Than Gold – the summer between their junior and senior years

This short story can be found in the CatholicTeenBook anthology, *Secrets: Visible and Invisible*. When the four teens volunteer together at a summer camp for disadvantaged kids, their week to help others turns into much more than they ever could have imagined. www.CatholicTeenBooks.com

Unlikely Witnesses – the summer between their junior and senior years

When four friends vacation together in the Colorado Rockies, they expect a week of hiking, biking, and rafting—not intense interrogations by the FBI. The fun and intrigue of this short story is paired with a reminder that if we live our lives as Christians, we never know when we might be a witness for Christ.

For information on my other faith-based YA novels, please visit my website or follow me on social media. God bless and happy reading!

Leslea Wahl

Website: www.LesleaWahl.com
Facebook: LesleaWahlBooks
Instagram: MinistryThruMystery and Blindside_Jake

CPSIA information can be obtained
at www.ICGtesting.com
Printed in the USA
FSHW011958310120
66501FS

9 781732 903715